"I'm sure Ms. Me... person, but we do... a man in the house and—"

"What luck!" Alex interrupted. He slid a possessive arm around Sierra's shoulders. "Sierra and I have decided to get married soon, and since we'd like to have children right off, having the baby here would be wonderful practice for both of us."

The woman's face brightened considerably. "You two are getting married?"

Sierra suspected she must look like a dying carp, so she snapped her mouth shut and tried to hide the shock rushing from her head to her feet. What was Alex doing telling this woman an out-and-out lie? she wondered wildly. He hated liars! And he hated the idea of marriage even more!

Dear Reader,

Celebrate those April showers this month by curling up inside with a good book—and we at Silhouette Special Edition are happy to start you off with *What's Cooking?* by Sherryl Woods, the next in her series THE ROSE COTTAGE SISTERS. When a playboy photographer is determined to seduce a beautiful food critic fed up with men who won't commit…things *really* start to heat up! In Judy Duarte's *Their Unexpected Family,* next in our MONTANA MAVERICKS: GOLD RUSH GROOMS continuity, a very pregnant—not to mention, single—small-town waitress and a globe-trotting reporter find themselves drawn to each other despite their obvious differences. Stella Bagwell concludes THE FORTUNES OF TEXAS: REUNION with *In a Texas Minute.* A woman who has finally found the baby of her dreams to adopt lacks the one element that can make it happen—a husband—or *does* she? She's suddenly looking at her handsome "best friend" in a new light. Christine Flynn begins her new GOING HOME miniseries—which centers around a small Vermont town—with *Trading Secrets,* in which a down-but-not-out native repairs to her hometown to get over her heartbreak…and falls smack into the arms of the town's handsome new doctor. *Least Likely Wedding?* by Patricia McLinn, the first in her SOMETHING OLD, SOMETHING NEW… series, features a lovely filmmaker whose "groom" on celluloid is all too eager to assume the role in real life. And in *The Million Dollar Cowboy* by Judith Lyons, a woman who's fallen hard for a cowboy has to convince him to take a chance on love.

So don't let those April showers get you down! May is just around the corner—and with it, six fabulous new reads, all from Silhouette Special Edition.

Happy reading!

Gail Chasan
Senior Editor

Please address questions and book requests to:
Silhouette Reader Service
U.S.: 3010 Walden Ave., P.O. Box 1325, Buffalo, NY 14269
Canadian: P.O. Box 609, Fort Erie, Ont. L2A 5X3

IN A TEXAS MINUTE

STELLA BAGWELL

SPECIAL EDITION

Published by Silhouette Books

America's Publisher of Contemporary Romance

If you purchased this book without a cover you should be aware that this book is stolen property. It was reported as "unsold and destroyed" to the publisher, and neither the author nor the publisher has received any payment for this "stripped book."

Special thanks and acknowledgment are given to Stella Bagwell for her contribution to THE FORTUNES OF TEXAS: REUNION series.

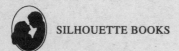 **SILHOUETTE BOOKS**

ISBN 0-373-24677-3

IN A TEXAS MINUTE

Copyright © 2005 by Harlequin Books S.A.

All rights reserved. Except for use in any review, the reproduction or utilization of this work in whole or in part in any form by any electronic, mechanical or other means, now known or hereafter invented, including xerography, photocopying and recording, or in any information storage or retrieval system, is forbidden without the written permission of the editorial office, Silhouette Books, 233 Broadway, New York, NY 10279 U.S.A.

All characters in this book have no existence outside the imagination of the author and have no relation whatsoever to anyone bearing the same name or names. They are not even distantly inspired by any individual known or unknown to the author, and all incidents are pure invention.

This edition published by arrangement with Harlequin Books S.A.

® and ™ are trademarks of Harlequin Books S.A., used under license. Trademarks indicated with ® are registered in the United States Patent and Trademark Office, the Canadian Trade Marks Office and in other countries.

Visit Silhouette Books at www.eHarlequin.com

Printed in U.S.A.

Books by Stella Bagwell

Silhouette Special Edition

Found: One Runaway Bride #1049
†*Penny Parker's Pregnant!* #1258
White Dove's Promise #1478
††*Should Have Been Her Child* #1570
††*His Defender* #1582
††*Her Texas Ranger* #1622
††*A Baby on the Ranch* #1648
In a Texas Minute #1677

Silhouette Books

The Fortunes of Texas
The Heiress and the Sheriff

Maitland Maternity
Just for Christmas

A Bouquet of Babies
†"Baby on Her Doorstep"

Midnight Clear
†"Twins under the Tree"

Going to the Chapel
"The Bride's Big Adventure"

Getaway
"Home on Leave"

Silhouette Romance

Golden Glory #469
Moonlight Bandit #485
A Mist on the Mountain #510
Madeline's Song #543
The Outsider #560
The New Kid in Town #587
Cactus Rose #621
Hillbilly Heart #634
Teach Me #657
The White Night #674
No Horsing Around #699
That Southern Touch #723
Gentle as a Lamb #748
A Practical Man #789
Precious Pretender #812
Done to Perfection #836
Rodeo Rider #878
Their First Thanksgiving #903
The Best Christmas Ever #909
New Year's Baby #915

Hero in Disguise #954
Corporate Cowgirl #991
Daniel's Daddy #1020
A Cowboy for Christmas #1052
Daddy Lessons #1085
Wanted: Wife #1140
†*The Sheriff's Son* #1218
†*The Rancher's Bride* #1224
†*The Tycoon's Tots* #1228
†*The Rancher's Blessed Event* #1296
†*The Ranger and the Widow Woman* #1314
†*The Cowboy and the Debutante* #1334
†*Millionaire on Her Doorstep* #1368
The Bridal Bargain #1414
Falling for Grace #1456
The Expectant Princess #1504
The Missing Maitland #1546
Because of the Ring #1589

*Heartland Holidays
†Twins on the Doorstep
††Men of the West

STELLA BAGWELL

sold her first book to Silhouette in November 1985. More than fifty novels later, she still loves her job and says she isn't completely content unless she's writing. Recently, she and her husband of thirty years moved from the hills of Oklahoma to Seadrift, Texas, a sleepy little fishing town located on the coastal bend. Stella says the water, the tropical climate and the seabirds make it a lovely place to let her imagination soar and to put the stories in her head down on paper.

She and her husband have one son, Jason, who lives and teaches high school math in nearby Port Lavaca.

Pssst, have you heard?
They're baaack!

Silhouette Special Edition presents three *brand-new* stories about the famous—and infamous!— Fortunes of Texas. Juicy scandals, heart-stopping suspense, love, loss… What else would you expect from the fabulous Fortunes?

Beginning in February 2005, read all about straitlaced CEO Jack Fortune and feisty Gloria Mendoza in RITA® Award-winning author Marie Ferrarella's *Her Good Fortune,* Special Edition #1665.…

Then, in March, Gloria's tell-it-like-it-is older sister, Christina Mendoza, finds herself falling hard for boss Derek Rockwell's charming ways, in Crystal Green's *A Tycoon in Texas,* Special Edition #1670.…

Finally, watch as youngest sister, Sierra, tries desperately to ignore her budding feelings for her best friend—and emotional opposite— Alex Calloway, in Stella Bagwell's April installment *In a Texas Minute,* Special Edition #1677.…

The Fortunes of Texas: Reunion—
The price of privilege. The power of family.

Chapter One

"Sierra! Hello! Are you there?"

Sierra Mendoza's gaze circled the table where she and her friends had gathered for lunch. Every eye was zeroed in on her and she suddenly realized her mind had wandered off again and she'd lost all train of the conversation.

Her cheeks pink with embarrassment, she glanced at Gayle, a blonde who was five years older than Sierra and much more experienced in the men department.

"I'm sorry, Gayle, I was…thinking about something. I didn't hear your question."

Gayle rolled her blue eyes, but softened the impatient gesture with a smile. "I asked if you wanted to try one of those fudge brownie desserts with me today?"

"Ugh, no. I—I'm just not in the mood for sugar today," she said, declining.

Actually Sierra wasn't in the mood for anything. She was only here at this lunch because these people were her best friends and had been since she'd met them at the University of Texas at Austin many years ago.

Today the two women and three men had congregated for their weekly lunch get-together at the Longhorn Bar and Grill in downtown Red Rock, Texas.

Back in San Antonio's earlier days, the Longhorn building had been a feed-and-grain store and today it was still more like a barn than anything else. The ceiling was high, open and crossed with heavy rafters. The wooden planked floor was rough and the pine picnic tables were covered with blue-and-white checked tablecloths. What used to be the loading dock was now an outside dining area that looked out over Main Street. The air in and out of the Longhorn always smelled of beer and fried onions, scents that mingled with laughter and rowdy conversation.

Mario, a Hispanic doctor who worked the emergency room in one of San Antonio's larger hospitals, turned a look of concern on Sierra. "What's the matter? Are you trying to diet? You certainly don't need to. You've gotten too thin in my opinion."

Feeling as if a bright spotlight were focused on her, Sierra dropped her gaze to the half-eaten lunch plate in front of her. "Not really, Mario. I've been eating plenty. I just don't want dessert today." She looked up and smiled apologetically at Gayle. "Maybe next week I'll have more of an appetite. Why don't you go ahead and eat one without me."

Laughing, Gayle shook her head. "No way. I'm not going to be the only one to eat a days' worth of calories in one small bowl."

"Well, I think Mario is right," Trey spoke up. "Sierra looks thin and pale. We've all noticed it. So what's wrong, honey? Still mooning over Chad Newbern?"

She looked at Trey, a big, brawny civil engineer with forearms the size of Popeye's and an even bigger heart.

"I don't want to talk about him," she said flatly.

She didn't even want to think about Chad, much less talk about him. Sierra had dated the man for two long years and then, suddenly, two months ago, he'd told her he wanted out of their relationship. He'd explained how he wanted more excitement in his life and Sierra was left with the clear conclusion that she'd simply been too boring to satisfy him. The whole incident had left her ego in shreds.

"Why not? It's obvious you're still thinking about the loser."

A grimace tightened her jaw as she looked directly across the table at Alex Calloway, the smooth lawyer of the bunch. A look of pure boredom etched his handsome features and Sierra had the most unladylike urge to kick his shins beneath the table. Of all her friends, Alex had a way of irritating her the most. Sarcasm should have been his middle name and there were times he could be so callous Sierra wanted to bop him over the head. Yet, on the other hand, he could turn around and be a real peach whenever he wanted to be.

Sierra had never considered him as more than a good friend and she supposed it was that complex personality of his that had kept her from falling for his tall, lanky good looks. And thank God for that, she thought. Alex was a heartbreaker of the worst kind.

"You don't know what I'm thinking," she bit sharply back at him.

"Well, I certainly believed old Chad was gonna be your husband someday soon. I was expectin' you to waltz in here and tell us wedding bells were fixin' to ring," Trey spoke up. "Instead the jerk runs out on you."

"Yeah. And after all you've done for the cad," Gayle added disgustedly. "There's nothing as sorry as a sorry man."

Trey scowled at Gayle, but none of the three men at the table bothered to speak up and defend their gender. Instead Mario looked sympathetically at Sierra and said, "Well, at least you got him off alcohol. And he's got a steady job. You can feel good about that."

"Yes, sir," Trey spoke up brightly, "you fixed Chad Newbern when he was pretty broken. You can feel proud of yourself for helping someone to get on with his life."

It was true that Sierra had been proud of the progress Chad had made since she'd first met him two years ago. At that time, he'd just been discharged from the navy for medical reasons and he'd been devastated over losing a career he'd wanted so badly. He'd taken to drinking to get the loss off his mind, until the liquor had taken hold of him.

Sierra had been touched by his wounded spirit and

slowly but surely she'd helped him get over the drinking problem. In the process, she'd fallen in love. And she supposed her biggest mistake had been thinking that Chad had fallen in love, too.

"Yeah," Alex drawled as he lifted his beer mug to his lips, "Sierra's not just a social worker, she's a miracle worker. She's good at patching things. No matter how rotten they are."

"Alex!" Gayle scolded. "Can't you see that Sierra is hurting? She needs our support."

A mocking slant spread over Alex's firmly chiseled lips. "What Sierra needs to do is stiffen her spine before someone else walks all over her."

Sierra gripped her beer mug with both hands and stared down at the thick sudsy bubbles as she did her best to blink back her tears. Maybe Alex was right, she thought with a sigh of defeat. It seemed as though every boyfriend she'd ever had in the past only stuck around long enough for Sierra to "fix" him, and then he was gone with the wind. What was wrong with her anyway? Didn't she have any lasting appeal to the opposite sex?

Straightening her shoulders as best she could, Sierra pinned her warm brown eyes on Alex's mocking face.

"Like you do to your opponents in the courtroom?" she asked coolly.

The mocking twist of his lips suddenly tilted upward to a droll smile. "You play the game to win, Sierra. You don't play it to lose."

For a moment awkward silence fell over the table, then finally Trey said, "Sierra, you're a beautiful young woman. You'll find the right man for you one of these days. Just keep that pretty little chin of yours up."

Sierra appreciated Trey's kindness, but she'd never gone so far as to think of herself as beautiful. Her sisters, Gloria and Christina, were beautiful. They were tall and willowy and sophisticated. Sierra barely measured five foot three. And though she was curvy, she was very petite. Many of her old high school friends still called her Runt and the long black mass of curls flying around her head didn't help her little-girl image.

"Thanks, Trey," she said. "But I don't think I'll be looking for a long, long while. Right after Chad and I broke up, I made a pact with my sisters. We all vowed to steer clear of men completely. If we broke our promise, we'd have to do some unholy task like mow the lawn or wash cars. Believe me, I'm not going to end up like Gloria and Christina. I plan to stick to my pledge."

"Oh, don't let this make you cynical," Mario spoke up. "Trey is right. You'll find the right person. Maybe tomorrow. Who knows?"

Mario was smiling at her with encouragement and she tried her best to smile back. Thankfully the waitress chose that moment to arrive with their food and the subject of Sierra's love life was dropped. She focused her attention on the meal as though she was thoroughly enjoying every bite.

However, she was relieved when the five of them said their goodbyes and she hurried across the parking lot to her waiting car. She wasn't in the mood for conversation with anyone. The spring afternoon was windy, but bright and warm. A walk in the park would do her good. But, at the moment, all she wanted to do was go home and cry her eyes out.

"Just a minute, Sierra. I want to talk to you."

Hearing Alex's voice right behind her, Sierra paused from opening the car door to turn and look at him. He was a tall man, at least six foot, with warm brown hair combed straight back from his forehead and clear green eyes that were usually glinting with a heavy dose of cynicism. He had the sort of hard, tough features that intimidated people, which she supposed was an asset in his line of work. Yet his face matched his lean, leathery body perfectly and, in spite of his lack of feelings at times, she had to admit he was a very attractive man.

"Why?" she quipped the question. "So you can stick the dagger in farther and twist it? I've really had enough, Alex."

Turning back to the car door, she jabbed the key in the lock and twisted it. Yet before she could pull the door open, Alex's hand was on her shoulder and she frowned as he tugged her back around to face him.

"No," he said in a voice as smooth as steel. "I don't think you've had nearly enough. It's ridiculous the way you were back there in the grill, crying into your beer like all your tomorrows have ended."

The disgust on his face not only hurt Sierra, it infuriated her and her pink lips parted as she stared up at him. "I wouldn't expect you to understand, Alex. You wouldn't know what love was, even if it gave you a good slap in the face."

He rolled his eyes and she breathed in a deep breath hoping it would calm her rising temper.

"Oh, please!" he groaned with disbelief. "You call what you had with Chad 'the loser' Newbern love? You needed to get rid of him ages ago. I'm glad he finally got enough sense to see it, too."

Her jaw clamped tight, Sierra turned her face away from his. "I'd really like to know who named you perfect man of the year," she said through gritted teeth. "Whoever it was had a screw loose."

"I don't profess to be perfect," he shot back at her.

Sierra's gaze flew up to his. "If you know so much about love, Counselor, why don't you have a woman draped permanently on your arm?"

His lean features scowled at her. "Maybe because I'm smart enough to realize that I don't need a woman just to make me happy. Hell, I don't even need one to help me stand upright. I can do that all by myself. The way you should be doing instead of clinging like a needy vine to every loser who comes along and gives you a second glance."

Pain ricocheted through her body. She was used to Alex being tough at times, but she wasn't ready for this kind of scolding. He was her friend, for Pete's sake. Couldn't he see she needed sympathy and understanding right now?

Swallowing at the knot of pain in her throat, she reached up and grabbed at the curls blowing into her misty brown eyes. "I've got to go, Alex."

"Not yet. I—"

"You've made your point." She shrugged her shoulder away from his hand. "I'm going home. I'll see you later," she said numbly, and before he could stop her she opened the car door and quickly slid behind the wheel.

Throwing up his hands with disgust, Alex stepped back and watched her drive out of the parking lot.

Damn man, Sierra thought as she drove through the residential streets of Red Rock. He could be so pompous at times that she wanted to slap him. But she couldn't help loving him as a friend. During college Sierra had gone through some rough ground. Alex had always been there to lend her a hand and keep her morale boosted. Then later, after college, when her two older sisters had become estranged from the family and each other, Sierra had been devastated. Being a social worker, she'd always believed she could help the most torn families get back together, but she'd not been able to make her sisters see eye to eye and that had left Sierra feeling even more useless. Alex had been around to promise her that things would get better. And they had.

Gloria and Christina had both come home to stay. Everyone was talking and laughing again. Gloria was pregnant with her first child and planning a June wedding with business magnate Jack Fortune. Christina had just announced her engagement to Derek Rockwell. Both her sisters were happy and in love.

Sierra had believed she would be the next in line. She'd been dreaming of going to her sisters and telling them that she, too, would soon be walking down the aisle. But that likelihood had ended, along with all the rest of her starry-eyed plans for the future.

Five minutes later, Sierra was trying not to think about anything pertaining to marriage as she turned down a neat residential street and parked in front of an old two-story house shaded in the front and the back by spreading live oaks.

A cattleman had built the house back in the 1880s. The story went that his wife had loved throwing parties and the couple had needed a second house in town to accommodate their guests. Down through the years, the owners of the house had changed, and modern bathrooms had been added, but basically the structure had remained the same. The floors were all polished oak and the walls and ceiling intricate tongue and groove.

The place needed a bit of repairs here and there and the board siding was faded to a chalky-white, but since the owner was an old friend of the family, Sierra got a great deal on the rent. And she loved the space and the character of the house, even if the old rooms seemed lonely at night.

Inside, she went straight to her bedroom and changed her printed cotton dress for a pair of blue jeans and a white T-shirt. After she'd slipped on a pair of loafers and tied her black curls into a ponytail, she went out to the living room to go through the mail she'd left stacked on an end table near the couch.

By now her earlier anger at Alex had dissolved and as she ripped into the envelopes, regret began to settle on her shoulders. Even if Alex had been nasty to her, he'd been doing it out of kindness. She shouldn't have been nasty back to him. That was beneath her usual demeanor and she hated that she'd lost her temper with him. Maybe she should give him time to get back to his office, then call and apologize, she pondered.

She was still debating whether to pick up the phone, when a knock sounded on the front door. Since she rarely had visitors in the middle of the afternoon, she was fully expecting to see a salesman when she opened the door. The last person she imagined to see standing on the porch was Alex Calloway.

"What are you doing here?" she asked bluntly.

With a slight grimace, he ran a hand through his brown hair. "May I come in?" he asked.

Sierra had already forgiven him, but she didn't want to be too quick in letting him know it. He was always accusing her of being too soft. Maybe now was the time to show him a tougher side of her.

"Why? So you can continue to insult me?"

His brows lifted and fell as he eyed her grim face. "No. And I don't want to have this conversation standing in the doorway."

Heaving out a breath, she pushed the screen door wide and gestured for him to come into the house. He walked to the middle of the room and jammed his hands into the pockets of his chinos. The khaki-colored pants were topped with a long-sleeved, dark green shirt and matching green tie flecked with spots of bright yellow. His clothing was far from the high-powered designer suits that were seen on many of the affluent lawyers in

San Antonio. But Alex wasn't into impressions, especially the outward kind. He was more interested in making his clients feel comfortable and gaining their confidence. That was something Sierra had always appreciated about him.

"I thought you had a client to meet with this afternoon. Isn't he waiting?" Sierra asked.

Alex was a trial lawyer with an office in San Antonio. Since he'd gotten his license to practice four years ago, he'd gone it alone, preferring to have his own business and do things his own way than to be a part of a large firm. Sierra admired his independence, but she often questioned him about the location of his office.

San Antonio was twenty miles away. Alex lived here in Red Rock. His hometown needed him much more than a city that was already full of lawyers.

"I told Pauline to keep him entertained until I got there," he answered. "She will."

Pauline was a perky, middle-aged woman who ran Alex's office single-handedly. The legal secretary was the only woman Sierra had ever met who could put Alex in his place. Yet he was always quick to sing Pauline's praises. Which was a smart thing on his part. Sierra seriously doubted he could find another paralegal who would put up with his demands.

Sierra went over to the couch and sank onto an end cushion. Since the day was warm but not hot, she'd opened the windows and turned on the ceiling fans. The blades far above Alex's head were turning in lazy, squeaky circles while beyond the window screens two mockingbirds jabbered at each other. It was a lazy, Texas afternoon, but at the moment every nerve in her body was focused on the male strutting back and forth in front of her.

"So, why are you here?" she asked again.

He paused to look at her. "To say I'm sorry and that I acted like a jerk to you."

Sierra was swamped with relief and she couldn't help but smile back at him. "You did act like a jerk, but I forgive you. Actually, about the time you knocked on the door, I'd decided I needed to call you to apologize. I wasn't exactly nice to you, either."

His hands still in his pockets, he walked over to the couch and took a seat next to her. "Forget it, Sierra. I just want you to—well, I don't like seeing you like this. We've been friends for years and how many times have I watched some good-for-nothing bum walk all over you? Too many," he added before she could answer. "They is right. You're a beautiful young woman, you shouldn't be settling for less."

Alex thought she was beautiful? He'd never said anything like that to her before! Alex had always had his pick of gorgeous women. To think that he'd even bothered to consider her looks was a shocker.

Feeling suddenly awkward, Sierra's gaze dropped to a spot on the floor. "Alex, I've never purposely set out to pick a loser for a boyfriend. It—it just turns out that way. I guess I just have horrible judgment of men."

She lifted her eyes to see him shaking his head. "Why do you even need a man in your life, Sierra?"

Gasping, she rolled her brown eyes toward the ceiling. "Are you crazy, Alex? I'm a woman and I have normal, healthy needs just like other women my age. We want affection, love and companionship in our lives. Let's face it. Living single gets pretty lonely at times. You should know that."

"Look, Sierra, there's nothing wrong with having a man around now and then. You just don't need to— well, long so much for wedding bells. I thought you women had moved beyond that old-fashioned notion of marriage, anyway."

She shook her head in dismay. "Alex, you just don't understand."

He arched an accusing brow at her. "It's your sisters who have you all upset. They're getting married in the next few months. And now your chance is gone because Chad, the loser, skipped out on you. That's what this is all about, isn't it?"

Feeling as though she were under a microscope, Sierra got to her feet and began to walk around the large, sparsely furnished room. "Maybe. Just a little," she mumbled. "For five years my sisters were both gone from home. Gloria lived in Colorado and Christina lived in California, but you know all of this. I've whined to you about it so many times before. You understand how much I missed them and how awful it was for my parents to lose two of their daughters."

Alex nodded. "I remember the rift between your sisters was awful—it tore your parents' hearts out to have the family broken in such a way. And all that time, you stayed behind and did your best to help your parents in any way they needed. Now your black-sheep sisters come home and smooth out their differences. All is well. They're forgiven. Both of them find the loves of their life."

"Yeah," Sierra tacked on with a measure of bitterness. "And me—the boring, good little daughter loses hers."

The last of her words were spoken in a choked voice and she paused at one of the open windows to compose herself.

Across the room, Alex cursed and jumped to his feet. "Hell's bells, Sierra! Chad wasn't the love of your life! You and I both know it!"

She glanced over her shoulder to see him striding toward her. His face was a picture of impatient disgust and she realized their conversation in the parking lot had suddenly come full circle.

"You don't know any such thing, Counselor."

His hand closed around her upper arm and as he looked down at her, his features gentled. "Yes, I do, honey. You've never had that look of love on your face. It hasn't happened yet."

Sierra's brown eyes widened. "You know how a woman in love looks?"

Suddenly he laughed and patted her cheek. "Is that a trick question, Sierra?"

She started to laugh with him, but the lighthearted moment quickly ended as another knock sounded on the front door.

Frowning, Alex glanced toward the front entrance. "Are you expecting someone?"

"No. It's probably a darn salesperson. Maybe you should go to the door, Alex. They don't like to deal with men."

He flashed her a confident smile. "Sure. I'll get rid of him real quick."

While Alex went to answer the door, Sierra decided to go into the kitchen and make a pot of coffee. She was halfway there when Alex turned away from the door and called to her.

"Sierra, I think you need to come here."

"Coming."

She joined Alex on the threshold and was surprised when she looked out onto the wide porch to see a teenage girl holding a newborn baby in a plastic carrier.

"Miss Sierra?" she asked in a small voice. "Is that you?"

"Yes." Sierra pushed the screen door open and stepped onto the porch for a better look at the timid teenager. "Is that you, Ginger?"

The young woman with short, chestnut hair and very pale skin nodded. At the same time Sierra recognized her from one of the families she'd visited as a social worker. Ginger Rollins. Her father had abused her mother and the courts had issued a restraining order against him. Now the mother was doing her best to care for three children. It was the same old refrain that Sierra saw over and over in her line of work. Only this time it was complicated even more by Ginger being pregnant with a child.

"Is something wrong? Has your dad moved back in the house?"

Ginger nervously shook her head. "No. I—see—I've had my baby. A boy."

Sierra stepped forward and peered down at the tiny infant. A fuzz of light, reddish-brown hair covered his head and although his eyes were closed in sleep, Sierra could see he was a handsome child with a sweet little bow mouth and a nose that was just big enough to look boyish.

"He's adorable, Ginger," Sierra exclaimed with a glowing smile for the baby. "You must be very proud."

"Yes, Miss Sierra. I am."

Sierra looked up at the girl's anxious face. "So what can I do for you, Ginger?"

Blushing, the teenager looked down at her baby and Sierra felt her heart jerk with sorrow. Mother and child both needed so much help if they expected to make it in this world. And where would they find it? Certainly not from her family, she thought sadly.

"I was wondering if you could babysit for me? Just for a little while," she added hastily. "You see, my mom's at work and I—need to go to the hospital. My aunt is there having some tests run and she's pretty scared and all. I thought I'd sit with her and try to make her feel a little better."

Sierra didn't hesitate. She had the rest of the day off. Having a baby in the house might be the very thing she needed to shake the depression she'd been feeling today.

"Why, of course," she told Ginger. "I'd be glad to watch him for you."

Smiling with relief, Ginger pushed the baby carrier

into Sierra's arms. "That'd be great! I'll go get his diaper bag from the car. I'll be back in a second."

"You're a real sucker for a manly face, aren't you?"

She glanced around to see that Alex had walked out onto the porch and was now peering over her shoulder at the baby.

"Well, I just couldn't resist this little man," she confessed. "Isn't he cute, Alex? Look, he's got a dimpled chin just like yours."

Alex chuckled. "Oh, no," he said wryly. "You won't ever see a baby with my genes stamped on his face. Kids are a serious responsibility. One that I'm not up to."

Sierra had never heard Alex say he was opposed to having children and she started to question him about his remark, but Ginger was returning with the diaper bag.

"Thank you, Miss Sierra," the teenager said with a breathless rush. "Everything that you need is in there. And I'll—be back as soon as I can."

"There's no need for you to hurry your visit, Ginger," Sierra assured her. "I hope you can help your aunt feel better. And your baby will be in good hands."

With a sheepish smile, Ginger jumped off the porch and hurried across the lawn to the curb where a rattletrap, hatchback car was waiting.

Thoughtfully, Sierra watched the girl pull onto the street and drive out of sight. "Looks like I've been handed a job for this afternoon," she said as she turned to go into the house.

Alex grabbed the diaper bag and followed her. "What's the baby's name?" he asked.

"Oh. I forgot to ask," Sierra told him. "But since he can't answer us, I guess it doesn't matter."

Her face glowing with excitement, she carried the baby over to the couch and placed him and the carrier onto the middle cushion. Alex sat down on the opposite side of the sleeping boy.

"He is cute," Alex admitted as he closely studied the baby. "Kinda bald, but I guess his hair will grow. Are all babies like that? With just a little bit of hair?"

Sierra's soft laugh was full of disbelief. "It amazes me that you're smart enough to pass the bar exam but you don't know anything about a baby."

"I'm smart enough to know that they're noisy and wet. And that so far I've been careful not to produce any."

She leaned back from the baby and folded her arms against her breasts. "And why is that, Alex?"

He shot her a tired look. "Isn't it obvious, Sierra? I'm not married. A kid needs a mom and a dad. Together in the same house. Instead of one living on the north side of town and one living on the south."

Her eyes slid over his rugged features as she imagined what a son of Alex's might be like. Strong, sturdy and handsome. He would raise a child of his with a firm but loving hand, just the way a father should be.

"Well, you've had plenty of offers for marriage," Sierra reminded him.

With a mocking laugh, he stood up. "Marriage is just something to keep divorce lawyers rich. I don't plan on contributing to their wealth."

"One of these days we're going to have to work on that cynical attitude of yours," Sierra told him.

He grinned. "Yeah. And one of these days you're going to learn to put some iron in that spine of yours." With a cocky wink, he started to the door. "I've got to get to work. Have a nice afternoon, little mother."

"I was going to make you some coffee," she called to him. "Now you're running off."

Shaking his head, he stepped onto the porch. "We'll do that some other time." He peered back at her through the screen. "You just take care of your little guy, there. And forget about that other one. Hear me?"

Hear him? He'd been giving her advice for years. Maybe it was time she listened to the bossy counselor.

"I'll try, Alex."

Chapter Two

Sierra was so fascinated by the baby that an hour passed before she realized she'd been sitting on the couch simply watching him sleep.

After a few more minutes, she forced herself to get up and go to the kitchen and began making that pot of coffee. While she was waiting for it to drip, the baby began to let out soft, intermittent cries.

Back in the living room, she carefully changed the baby's diaper and then fed him the formula that Ginger had left in the diaper bag. He went back to sleep soon after he drank a portion of the bottle and Sierra lay him on her bed so that he'd be out of the afternoon breeze wafting through the living room windows.

While the baby slept, Sierra couldn't help wondering about the tot's name and how Ginger and her mother were going to care for him when they now had five mouths in the house to feed. There were programs for the needy that would help. Sierra was going to make a point to go by the Rollinses' house and make sure Mrs. Rollins took advantage of the aid. She also wanted to make sure that Mr. Rollins wouldn't be coming around in a drunken stupor and swinging his fist at anyone who stepped in front of him.

Another hour passed and then two more. And though she was enjoying every minute with the baby, Sierra couldn't help but wonder what was keeping Ginger. Four hours had passed since she'd dropped the child off and she'd not heard a word from her.

Deciding she'd better try to make contact, she called Red Rock General and asked them to page Ginger. After a long wait on hold, the switchboard operator came back on the line.

"I'm sorry, Miss Mendoza. The person isn't responding. She must have left the hospital."

Sierra's heart sank. "Oh. Well, could you tell me if you have a Mrs. Rollins listed?"

"Sure. Just a moment."

Sierra looked at the sleeping baby while she waited for an answer. Why would Ginger have stayed away this long? Why would she have simply left the newborn with her?

"Sorry, Miss Mendoza. There's no one been admitted by that name. Is there another name she might be listed under?"

Sierra had no idea what Ginger's maternal aunt's name might be so she simply thanked the operator and hung up.

What in the world was she going to do now? she wondered, call child care services? No. Because the Rollinses' home wasn't exactly fit for a newborn, they would probably take him straight to a foster home, or even worse an orphanage until something could be decided about his future. She couldn't bear the thought of this little guy being handed from one person to the next.

Worried now, Sierra began to pace the living room. While she'd been on the phone to the hospital, the sun had set and long shadows from the live oaks had settled over the front of the house. She switched on a lamp to chase away the gloom, then sat down next to the baby.

Maybe she should call her own parents, Sierra considered. But Jose and Maria couldn't do any more than she was already doing. And anyway, they were always scolding her for taking on everyone else's problems. They would definitely see "baby" as a huge problem. On top of that, her parents were usually at Red, the restaurant they owned, this time of the evening, eating or generally seeing that everything was running smoothly.

Sierra was acquainted with Wyatt Grayhawk, the sheriff of Red Rock. She should probably call him and report the baby as abandoned. But Wyatt was a tough stickler for the law and he would insist that the baby be taken to the proper authorities. She could already hear him saying that would be the right thing to do.

But every time Sierra looked at the baby's sweet, innocent face, she felt a fierce sense of protectiveness. She wanted to make sure he was loved, not just cared for.

Alex! She'd call Alex, Sierra suddenly decided. He was her friend and a lawyer; he'd weigh both sides of the situation for her.

At the same time, in San Antonio, Pauline, Alex's paralegal, marched into his office.

"Alex, what in hell are you doing? Your client just walked out the door. And he wasn't just angry. He was furious. He slammed the door so hard as he was leaving I thought the windows were going to shatter."

Leaning back in a large, black leather desk chair, Alex looked at his secretary who was leaning over his desk, waiting to hear a logical reason for the storm that had just blown from the office.

"It's simple, Pauline. I wouldn't take his case."

The graying brunette shot him a droll look. "I gathered that much, Alex. I want to know why? The man has money. He could have paid some bills around here. You know his father owns that construction firm that's building the fancy new row of shops out by the interstate."

"I don't care if his father is building a new mansion up at Crawford for the president. He's guilty. And you know my rules about taking cases. If I'm not totally sure the person is innocent, forget it."

Pauline straightened away from his desk and walked over to a coffeemaker situated in one corner of the small office. As she poured the brown liquid into a foam cup she said, "Well, it would be nice to stay on speaking terms with the electric company. We might need some light around here to get any work done."

Alex was more amused than anything by his secretary's comment. "I have plenty of candles at home. If need be, I'll bring them to work."

Pauline leveled a wry look at him as she carefully sipped her coffee. "It's April. Texas is starting to heat up. What are we going to do for air-conditioning?"

Alex batted a dismissive hand in her direction. "Hand fans. You can buy one for a dollar or two."

Pauline let out a mocking laugh. "Oh, that'd be real pleasant. What do you intend to do, sweat the truth out of your potential clients?"

"Very funny, Pauline. You know that we have plenty in the coffers to pay the electric bill. Don't try to make me feel guilty that I decided not to represent that bum."

Rising to his feet, he went over and poured himself a cup of coffee and added a measure of powdered creamer.

As he thoughtfully stirred his drink, Pauline said, "I always thought it was every person's right to have representation in court."

"Hmm. It is. He'll just have to find it somewhere else."

Seeing he'd made up his mind about the issue, Pauline said, "Okay. The bum was your last appointment for today. You've got a court date in the morning. Do you want to go over your opening argument?"

Alex shook his head. "No. I'm going to wait and let it all come from here." He tapped the spot on his chest that covered the region of his heart.

"All right. Do you want to go over your notes with me?"

Seeing she was intent on staying busy, Alex gave in. "Sure. Get the things. It never hurts to know every little detail of the case."

Pauline started out of the room to fetch the files, when the telephone rang. On her way toward the door, she stopped by one corner of Alex's desk and picked up the receiver.

After a brief exchange of words, she held the phone out to her boss. "It's Sierra."

Alex's brows shot up with surprise. Sierra rarely called him at work. And since he'd just left her house after lunch, he couldn't imagine what she might have to say to him.

Pauline jabbed the phone at Alex as though he needed to wake up. "You know, Sierra, the pretty young Hispanic woman who comes by and sees you from time to time."

Scowling impatiently at his secretary, he jerked the phone from her hand. "Yes, I know. And you can shut the door behind you!"

Pauline merely laughed as she left the room. Alex waited for the woman to close the door and then he sank onto his desk chair.

"Sierra, what's up?"

Sierra seemed to breathe a sigh of relief at the sound of his voice. "I'm sorry to bother you like this, Alex. I realize it's late and you're probably getting ready to head home, but I just had to speak to you. You're the only person I could think of to call about this."

Picking up on the panicked sound of her voice, Alex leaned forward, his expression alert. "What is 'this'?"

For some crazy reason, Sierra felt a ball of tears rushing to her throat. "It's the baby, Alex. Ginger never came back to get him."

"What do you mean, never came back? You haven't heard from her?"

Sierra gripped the receiver. "No. I tried to contact her at the hospital, but apparently she wasn't there. And now I have a sneaking suspicion the visit to her aunt was just a fabrication. Alex, I don't know what to do!"

Alex rose to his feet. "Sierra," he stressed with calm patience. "It's simple. You've got to call the authorities."

"No! I mean—not right now. Please, can you come over? I need to talk to you about this."

His first instinct was to yell at her, to order her to get off the phone and call the sheriff. But something about the desperate note in her voice stopped him. She'd just gone through a big disappointment with that Chad guy. And Alex had already given her enough rough treatment for one day. It wouldn't hurt if a little more time passed before she had to deal with the authorities.

"All right, Sierra. Sit tight and I'll be right over."

Alex hung up the phone and as he hurried out of the building, he ordered Pauline to close up and go home.

As he drove the twenty miles back to Red Rock, he kept thinking about Sierra. Ever since their college days, he'd considered her a close friend. She'd been an attractive woman when they'd walked the Texas University campus, and Alex couldn't deny that she'd grown even more beautiful these past few years. But he was smart enough to know that the two of them would never be compatible. She was too much of a Florence Nightingale and he—well, he had his own demons to deal with.

Sierra was walking the floor waiting for Alex to arrive when the baby started to whimper again. Taking a seat on the couch, she cradled him in her arms and then reached for the diaper bag sitting nearby. She remembered one more bottle being inside. Once that was gone, she'd have to see about getting more.

Whoa, Sierra. This baby isn't yours. Don't start letting yourself think in those terms.

Pressing her lips together in firm conviction, Sierra began to dig through the items in the baby bag. She pulled out a clean diaper and was fishing around for the bottle of formula when her hand came in contact with a piece of paper.

Pulling it from the bag, she could see it was a piece of lined notebook paper. The side facing her was blank, so she flipped it over and just as quickly reared back with shock. It was a short note:

Dear Miss Sierra,

I guess by now you've figured out that I'm leaving the baby with you. You've always been good to me and I know you'll love him and take good care of him. You'll give him the sort of home that I never could.

I've always wanted to go to California so that's where I'm headed. I want to find a better life for myself.
Ginger

Just then Sierra heard Alex parking his SUV in front of her house and she ran out onto the porch and across the yard to meet him.

"Oh, Alex! You're not going to believe this! I can hardly believe it myself. And I don't know what to do! You've—"

Alex grabbed her by the upper arms as she did a frantic dance on her toes.

"Whoa, honey. Just calm down. Where's the baby?"

A breath rushed out of her. "On the couch. Asleep. He just downed the last bottle."

Alex's arm slipped around her waist as he urged her toward the house. "Come on. Let's go in and you can tell me all about it."

Just having Alex near was enough to soothe her frayed nerves. By the time they entered the living room and took seats on the couch, her body had begun to relax somewhat.

"Okay. Start from the beginning and don't leave anything out," Alex instructed.

Sierra rolled her eyes. "Dear God, do you always have to be such a—lawyer?" She reached and collected a piece of paper from the coffee table. "Just read this. It explains most everything."

Alex took the note and quickly read through the carefully printed words. When he looked up at Sierra, his green eyes were as hard as stone.

"She just left him. Without a backward glance. Why doesn't that surprise me?"

The cold irony in his voice stunned Sierra. Alex had dealt with all sorts of crimes in his profession. He was used to seeing human nature at its worse and for the most part he took it all in stride.

"Alex! You're making Ginger sound like—a murderer, or worse!" Sierra gasped.

Rising, Alex went over to the baby and gazed down at his sleeping face. As Sierra watched a muscle tick in his jaw, she realized that this whole situation had brought painful memories back to him.

"Can you think of anything worse than abandoning your own child?" he asked sharply.

Her face full of concern, she got to her feet and laid a gentle hand on his arm. "Alex, I'm—sorry," she said softly. "I shouldn't have involved you."

A tight grimace etched his rugged features and then just as quickly the pained expression disappeared and he shook his head. "Forget it, Sierra. I came here to help you. Not to condemn anybody."

When Sierra's sisters, Gloria and Christina, had been gone from the family and her parents had constantly fretted about their welfare, she'd often lamented her worries to Alex. During one of those times, he'd surprised her by saying that at least Sierra knew who her real parents and siblings were.

Sierra had pressed him to explain the comment and he'd eventually confessed that, when he was thirteen, he'd discovered his adoption papers among his parents' important documents. Mitch and Emily Calloway had never told Alex that he was their adopted son. They'd always led him to believe that he'd been born to them right there in a Dallas hospital.

Alex had confronted the couple with the adoption papers and he'd eventually learned that his biological mother had left him on the steps of a human services building in Dallas. He'd only been two days old at the time. The truth had shaken the very foundation beneath Alex's feet and Sierra wasn't at all sure that he'd ever made peace with the circumstances of his birth.

"If it's too upsetting to you—"

"Sierra! I'm here. And I said forget it. Okay?"

Biting down on her lip, she studied him with worried brown eyes. Alex groaned and reached for her hand.

"Sierra," he said, his tone suddenly gentle. "It's all right. I'm a big boy. You don't have to worry about me."

The touch of his fingers wrapped around hers was strong and warm and comforting. Sierra unconsciously tightened her hand around his. "All right. So what do you advise me to do, Counselor?"

"Does Ginger have a family?"

"Yes. But the father has a restraining order against him. He drinks. And if he lives in the same house with the family, he beats on the mother and the children. Mrs. Rollins is trying to make a living for herself and her other children without him. There's no way she is capable of caring for an infant. She's just an inch away from having her own children taken away from her."

"Sounds like a lovely home life," Alex said, his voice dripping with sarcasm.

She sighed. "People can get themselves in some real predicaments, Alex. We're not all perfect and at least Mrs. Rollins is trying to overcome her mistake of a bad marriage."

Shaking his head, he pulled away from her and walked across the room. "God, Sierra, that soft heart of yours is going to get you into big trouble someday. Not everybody in this world has good in them, you know."

He was standing at one of the open windows, his forearm resting against the wooden seal as he looked out at the darkening night. Sierra left the couch and went to him.

"Alex, Ginger wanted me to have this baby. The note plainly says so. Doesn't that mean anything?"

His eyes widened in complete disbelief. "Are you telling me you want to keep the baby? Is that what this is all about?"

A pleading expression crossed her face as she held her hands outward and upward. "Alex, I don't want the boy to go to some orphanage or foster home."

He stabbed a forefinger toward the couch where the infant was quietly sleeping. "That little guy doesn't have any attachment to you."

Lifting her chin with defiance, she said, "Maybe not yet. But he will. And I *know* I can take wonderful care of him."

"Okay. Okay. I don't see any problem with you being

a foster mother. But as for Ginger's note, I'm not so sure it would stand up in a court of law. You'll have to become his foster mother on your own merit."

Sierra breathed a bit easier. She didn't know why the baby had become so important to her. She'd only had him with her for a few hours. And babysitting was nothing new for her. Friends were often asking Sierra to watch their children and not once during those occasions had she felt the sudden, unshakable attachment as she had with this little guy.

Her smooth brow puckered with concern. "Do you think that's possible? Child care services are so picky."

His lips slanted wryly. "We won't know until we talk with them," he said and before she could reply he started to the phone. "Where's your directory?"

Sierra found the book for him and stood anxiously aside as she waited for him to make the call.

After what seemed like an eon had passed, Alex finally hung up the phone and looked up at her. "Someone will be here within the hour. While we wait, why don't we have some coffee?"

Nodding numbly, Sierra started toward the kitchen. "You watch the little guy," she told him. "I'll bring the coffee in here when it's ready."

Alex opened his mouth to protest, but he closed it just as quickly. The baby was asleep. He wouldn't have to do anything. And Sierra was already in enough turmoil without him riling her with what she would consider foolishness on his part.

Besides, he didn't want to explain to her that it bothered him to be around babies. Or maybe she'd already guessed that. She'd apologized for bringing him into this situation. Apparently she'd realized Ginger's behavior had reminded him of his own biological mother. Damn the woman, wherever in the world she was. She'd not wanted Alex any more than Ginger had wanted the precious little life sleeping on Sierra's couch.

Tentatively he walked over to the baby and stared down at him. He was a handsome guy with thick lush lashes resting on his rosy cheeks. His arms and legs were long, predicting a tall man, while his chest promised to be wide and strong. His tiny lips made sucking movements and Alex was suddenly struck by the baby's total innocence, the overwhelming need for someone to nurture and care for him.

Sierra would be a good mother. He didn't have to think twice about that. But did he want to see her get mixed up with someone else's child? Did he want to see her get tangled up with any child?

"I'm sorry, Miss Mendoza, but our first obligation is to place this child with its own family. I'll need to make a concerted effort to find the birth mother."

Sierra swiped a hand across her forehead as she looked at the woman sitting in the armchair. Nancy Williams was a large, older lady with weary blue eyes and graying brown hair. She looked exhausted and Sierra figured she'd been in and out of several homes today. Places that weren't really homes but had to be inspected as such.

"Mrs. Williams, when you read the Rollins file, you'll see that placing the baby in that home is impossible. There's no doubt in my mind that he'd be neglected."

"I'll read the file Monday," the woman promised. "As for now, the sheriff needs to be contacted and the baby placed in a foster home until we can locate Ginger Rollins."

Sierra darted a look at Alex, who was sitting close beside her on the couch. Thank God, he'd never left her side since the woman had arrived. Right now she needed his strength.

"Why?" Sierra asked. "I'm perfectly capable of caring for the child. I can be his foster mother."

The child care worker's smile was too patronizing to hold any sort of warmth. "I'm certain you've never been a foster mother before, Miss Mendoza. And we have several homes with openings now. It won't be a problem to place the baby in one of them."

Sierra wanted to throw herself against Alex's chest and cling to him for dear life. He couldn't allow this woman to take the baby away. He just couldn't.

Reaching for his hand, she gripped it tightly and said, "I may not have been a foster mother before, but I have taken care of children. I can give him a good home."

"Miss Mendoza—"

"Look, Mrs. Williams," Alex suddenly interrupted the woman. "Sierra has worked for several years as a social worker. She understands what it takes to make a home for a child. Along with that, she's an upstanding member of the community. She's lived here in Red Rock all of her life and her parents own a popular eating establishment here in town. I can assure you she can produce excellent references to her character."

The woman studied the two of them for a moment, then let out a long breath as though she'd carefully considered the situation and hated to deliver her decision.

"Well," she began, "I'm sure Miss Mendoza is a reputable person, but we do like for there to be a man in the house and—"

"What luck," Alex interrupted again. He slid a possessive arm around Sierra's shoulders. "Sierra and I have decided to get married soon and since we'd like to have children right off, having the baby here would be wonderful practice for both of us."

The woman's face brightened considerably. "You two are getting married?"

Nodding, Alex answered without hesitation. "Yes. And if you need my references, I practice law in San Antonio. You can either call my office or stop by."

Sierra suspected she must look like a dying carp, so she snapped her mouth shut and tried not to hide the shock rushing from her head to her feet. What was Alex doing telling this woman an out-and-out lie? she wondered wildly. He hated liars! And he hated the idea of marriage even more!

Chapter Three

"Oh, well, that changes the whole situation," Nancy Williams said. "I'm sure there will be no problem for you to keep the baby here with the two of you. I'll notify the authorities of the child's whereabouts. And later, on Monday, I'll need for you to come down to our offices and sign some papers. Say, around ten o'clock in the morning?"

"I have to be in court Monday morning. Can we make it in the afternoon?" Alex asked.

Smiling wanly, the woman rose to her feet. "I'm sure that will be fine, Mr. Calloway. I'll call Miss Mendoza with a time." She turned a serious look on Sierra. "If you start having reservations about this, don't hesitate to call. Here's my card."

She placed it on the coffee table and Sierra left the couch to see the woman to the door. After another round of thank-yous and goodbyes, Sierra closed the door behind Nancy Williams and rushed out of the small foyer and into the living room where Alex still sat beside the baby.

"Alex! What has come over you? Are you taking some sort of mood-altering drug? Or have you and Pauline been having afternoon tequilas?"

Alex chuckled as he watched Sierra come to a screeching halt in the middle of the room and plant her fists on both sides of her hips.

"I'll have you know that I'm completely sober."

Her hands flew helplessly up in the air as she shook her head with disbelief, then tossed a hank of tangled black curls away from her face. "You're sober," she repeated with a sardonic roll of her eyes. "And you sat there and lied like a sneaky dog—implying to that woman that we are engaged and want children! What came over you anyway?"

Alex couldn't possibly tell Sierra what had come over him. Frankly, he didn't know. He was almost as stunned as Sierra was by his behavior. Yet now that it was done, he felt happy about the sudden impulse, as though something inside him was saying his intervention with a little white lie had been the right thing to do.

"What are you yapping about?" he countered. "It worked, didn't it? You got to keep the little guy. He's not going to an orphanage or a foster home. At least for now."

A pent-up breath rushed out of her and as it did she suddenly felt exhausted. The day had been a rollercoaster ride and now Alex was acting so out of character she was actually worried about him.

Going to the couch, she eased down next to him and laid a palm on his forehead. "You can't be well. Even on the most sane day of your life, you'd never tell anyone you were getting married."

"Bull," he said with a shrug, then turned his gaze on the baby. "What difference is it going to make what I told that woman? She's not going to bug this place with a camera."

Sierra noticed, not for the first time this evening, that Alex's features softened whenever he looked at the baby. There was a tenderness in his eyes that she'd never seen before and she had to admit she was very drawn to this new side of her friend.

"No," Sierra reluctantly agreed. "But eventually she, or someone else like her, will be back here to check up on us. They'll know that we aren't married. That we're not even living together!"

Turning his attention back to Sierra, Alex leaned over and grasped her by the upper arms. "We'll deal with that when the time comes. Besides, by that time you'll probably be ready to place the child in a good foster home."

Sierra didn't think so. But she wasn't going to argue with Alex tonight. He was right. For now everything was okay and she needed to leave it at that.

Closing her eyes, she nodded. "I'm sorry, Alex. I didn't mean to get so carried away." She looked at him as a weak smile slanted her rosy-pink lips. "And I do thank you so very much for stepping in and convincing Mrs. Williams to let me keep the baby."

Releasing his hold on her arms, he reached up and patted her cheek. "No need to thank me, kiddo. We're friends. We're supposed to help each other."

In Sierra's opinion what he'd done was above and beyond the call of friendship, but she wasn't going to point that out to him. The whole idea of them being engaged, even in a fake way, had left her feeling awkward and acutely aware of Alex's hand touching her cheek, his thigh pressing into hers.

Her throat suddenly tightened and she swallowed as her gaze dropped to her lap. "I couldn't think of anyone else to call but you. It means a lot to me that you came running."

He didn't reply immediately and she lifted her gaze to see he was thoughtfully studying her.

"Don't get soppy on me, Sierra. You know I'm not worth it," he said, then rose to his feet and walked over to a small table where he'd left his coffee cup. Picking it up, he asked, "What are you going to call him?"

"The baby?"

He cocked an eyebrow in an arrogant, upward slant. "That is what this is all about, isn't it?"

Knowing her cheeks were turning pink and hating him for it, she pushed herself up from the couch and walked over to where he stood.

"You can be a real ass, Alex."

"If I was any other way, no one would recognize me," he said, then smiled to buffer his words.

She groaned, but stopped herself from saying anything. From the first time she'd met Alex, nearly nine years ago, she could see he was wearing a callous, who-gives-a-damn cloak around him. But there were times that the cloak cracked just enough for her to see inside the man and she'd learned he had a big heart that was very capable of being broken. No one else but Sierra seemed to see this about Alex Calloway, the successful trial lawyer. And she supposed that was a major reason she did her best to overlook his sarcastic veneer. She knew there was far more to the man than the slick words that came out of his mouth.

"I don't know what to call him. Whatever he was named before—well, that life for him is over. He needs to start new with a whole new name. Got any ideas?" she asked.

Alex started to remind her that whatever she decided to call the baby would only be temporary. Just like her custody of him would only be temporary. But she seemed so happy about her new little charge, he couldn't bring himself to burst her bubble.

What the hell has come over you, Calloway? You take one look at a woman with a baby in her arms and you get soft as cornmeal mush.

Shaking away that disgusting thought, Alex said, "What about Bowie? After real Texas hero, Jim Bowie."

Sierra's brown eyes widened as she rolled the names over her tongue. "Jim Bowie. Bowie. Yes, that's nice and strong. Bowie—" She paused abruptly and shrugged. "Well, I guess we can't pin a last name on him. But Bowie will be enough for now."

As if he seemed to know he was being discussed, the

baby began to stir. By the time Sierra reached him, he was squalling at the top of his lungs and punching the air with two tight little fists.

"What's the matter with him?" Alex asked.

Sierra felt the baby's diaper. It was wet so she immediately sat down on the couch to change it. "This is the last diaper I have," Sierra said. "And I gave him the last bottle right before you came. I'm going to have to go to the store tonight and buy some baby supplies. Do you think you could help me?"

"Tonight! I've got to be in court by eight o'clock in the morning," Alex exclaimed loud enough to be heard above the baby's crying. "I've got notes to make and—"

"All right," Sierra abruptly interrupted. "Sorry I asked."

With a shake of his head, Alex headed toward the kitchen with his empty coffee cup. After a couple minutes, he returned and stood in the middle of the living room, his arms folded against his chest.

"You're really pushing our friendship, Sierra, you know that, don't you?" She didn't answer immediately and he groaned with surrender. "Okay, so I did offer to help you out."

She tried not to smile as she carefully placed the baby against her shoulder. He squirmed and then instantly quieted as she patted his back. "It's just one evening out of your busy life, Alex. And little Bowie will thank you for it later."

"Damn it," he said with a scowl. "Get whatever you need and let's go before I change my mind."

A few minutes later, as they neared the end of Austin Street and were about to turn onto Main, Sierra said, "Alex, would you please drive out to that new grocery store on the west side of town? I don't want to go to Bailey's. Everybody in there knows me."

Behind the wheel, Alex glanced at her as he braked to a stop at the intersection. "So? What's wrong with that?"

Tilting her head back and forth, she tried to explain without sounding insulting. "Well, you're with me."

"So?" he repeated. "Do I look like I'm diseased or something? The last I heard Bailey's hadn't barred lawyers from shopping there."

Frustration pushed a moan past her lips. "Oh, Alex, you know what I'm talking about. They'll think something is fishy. Me and you and a baby. Talk will be all over Red Rock."

"Sierra," he said with exaggerated patience. "We just told a child care worker that we planned to get married. The sooner that gossip gets around, the better."

She looked at him, her expression horrified. "No! Alex, my parents. I could never deceive them like that. There's already been too much miscommunication in my family."

"All right. All right. Explain to them what's going on, but make them promise to keep it quiet until little Bowie finds another home. Otherwise you might as well kiss him goodbye right now."

Sierra glanced over her shoulder at the baby strapped safely in his car seat. Funny how Bowie was already starting to feel like hers, she thought with a sting of emotional tears. And wasn't it even more odd to think of Alex as his father? Bowie Calloway. The name had a very nice ring to it even if she didn't have one on her finger.

The next afternoon, Sierra surprised her parents by showing up on their front porch with little Bowie in her arms. She'd dressed him in a pair of blue shorts and matching striped T-shirt, just one of the sets of clothing that she and Alex had purchased last night on their shopping spree for the baby. She'd combed Bowie's hair with just enough oil to make it lay to one side and tied a pair of tiny tennis shoes on his feet. He looked adorable and Sierra could see from the light in her mother's eyes that she was instantly taken with the baby.

"Sierra, where in the world did you get such a precious baby?"

Maria Mendoza leaned over Bowie for a closer look at the baby. Meanwhile Jose had come to the door to see who'd been ringing the bell. When he spotted Sierra and the baby, he joined them on the porch.

"A cute little boy," he remarked. "Who are you babysitting for, Sierra?"

Sierra looked from her father to her mother. The couple had been deeply in love for more than thirty years and that love had kept them both young and vibrant, even through the trying times. At sixty-two, Maria had the svelte, curvy body of a woman twenty years younger. Her rosy-tan skin glowed with scarcely a wrinkle and her black hair was streaked with only a small amount of gray. She was still quite a beautiful woman and made a perfect partner for Jose, who in Sierra's opinion had to be the most handsome, distinguished man in all of Red Rock.

Her father was a tall, strongly built man with black hair that had yet refused to gray, even though he had reached the age of sixty-five. He adored his wife and children and Sierra had often wished she could find a man in her life who was even half as wonderful as her father.

"Actually I'm not babysitting," Sierra told the both of them. "I've become Bowie's foster mother."

"You what?" This was from Jose.

At the same time, her mother exclaimed by practically shouting her name, "Sierra!"

"Let's go into the house," Sierra suggested. "The mosquitoes are out today and I don't want Bowie to get bit."

Her parents hurried their daughter into the house and hovered over her as she went into the kitchen and placed Bowie, strapped in his carrier, on the dining table.

"Now what is this about being a foster mother?" Jose demanded.

Rolling her eyes and shaking her head, Maria sank weakly onto one of the wooden chairs surrounding the table. "Sierra! A baby isn't like a stray cat or sick puppy!"

Sierra tried to hide her disappointment as her gaze took in both parents. She'd been hoping the two of them would be happy about the baby. But in all honesty, she hadn't really expected a joyous reaction from them. For some reason, maybe because she was the youngest of their three daughters, they'd always considered her their little girl instead of a grown woman. Even when she'd been dating Chad and talking of marriage, they had always dismissed her plans, certain that she would break up with him. Well, that part of their opinion about her had been right. She had broken up with Chad. But if they thought, for one minute, that baby Bowie was just a whim with her, then they were going to be in for a surprise.

"Mother, I do know the difference between a child and an animal!"

Maria waved a scoffing hand at Sierra. "Oh, you know what I mean. You've always taken in stray animals. And even needy friends at times. But a baby is a huge responsibility."

Stepping forward, Jose thoughtfully rubbed his jaw as he inspected Bowie's sleeping face.

"Your mother is right, honey. You have a job that takes up nearly all your time and—"

"I'm going to take a leave of absence for a month or two. I have enough money saved. And my position at work will be there when I'm ready to go back. I've already discussed it with my superiors."

Jose's black brows lifted as he shared a look of surprise with his wife.

"You've already made these decisions?"

Sierra nodded. "I know this all sounds sudden. But, frankly, everything happened at once. The baby was left with me at my house. Abandoned. And the mother wants me to have him."

Shocked, Maria's hand crept to her open mouth. Jose clucked his tongue with dismay.

"Sierra, your job—you see such horrible things. A woman giving up her own baby! What kind of person is this?" her father asked.

"A desperate teenager, Daddy. She has no husband and her father beats her and her mother."

Closing his eyes, Jose placed a hand against his forehead and shook his head. "Dear God, such evilness!"

Maria said, "There has to be more to it than just this girl wanting you to have the baby. There are laws and regulations about these things. What—"

"I've already spoken to child care services. Alex and I have to go to their offices in San Antonio in about an hour and sign some papers."

A curious frown wrinkled Jose's dark features. "Alex? Alex Calloway? Is he acting as your lawyer or something?"

Sierra cleared her throat. "Uh, no. Not exactly. We— uh, we told the child care worker that we were getting married so that little Bowie would have two parents."

Aghast, Maria shot up from her chair. "Married! Sierra, what were you thinking?"

"Are you two getting married?" Jose asked in a far more normal tone than his wife had spoken.

Sierra wasted no time in shaking her head. "Of course not. He—he's just helping me out with this. Because he knows I want to keep Bowie. At least for a while." She turned pleading eyes on her parents. "Please. Both of you, please, keep this to yourselves. Alex and I want everyone to think we're getting married. Otherwise—well, there might be all sorts of problems."

Maria groaned. "And you think lying will keep trouble from happening? That's not logical, Sierra."

Bowie chose that moment to wake up. As he began to squirm and open his eyes, Sierra reached down and picked him up from his carrier. The slight weight of his body cradled against her breast felt good and right. But she doubted her parents would understand her maternal feelings.

"Alex and I aren't lying, Mother. We're just pretending a bit. There can't be any harm in that. The two of us have been good friends for years. We understand each other. Believe me, there won't be any problems."

Maria and Jose exchanged worried glances while Sierra checked her wristwatch.

"I'm sorry, you two, but I've got to be going," Sierra apologized. "Alex is going to be expecting us at his office in about thirty minutes. And I might run into traffic."

Picking up the plastic carrier with one hand, Sierra turned and started out of the room. Her parents followed close on her heels.

"But what about your sisters?" Maria asked in a frantic rush. "What are we supposed to tell them?"

"That Alex and I are taking care of a baby for the next few weeks. That's all they need to know."

Daughter and parents reached the front entrance to the house and Jose laid a gentle hand on Sierra's shoulder.

"Where is this all going to lead, Sierra? I can't see anything permanent. And if you become attached to Bowie it could become very painful for you. Are you sure you want to go through such trauma? After all, you've just had this breakup with Chad."

"Your father is right, honey," Maria added. "If you're clinging to this child because you miss Chad, then you're doing it for the wrong reasons."

"Chad isn't even in the picture now," she said and realized with a start that she really meant it. Chad had been a bad mistake, nothing more. Strange that it had taken little Bowie and a few words from Alex to make her see that.

"Well, you certainly seemed all cut up about him a couple months ago. When you first told us about the breakup," Maria countered.

Sierra smiled broadly and marveled that she felt so lighthearted, so good today. Alex had been right all along. She'd not needed Chad "the loser" Newbern to make her happy.

"I was in a mild state of shock, Mother. But that's passed. And don't worry, you two, I can handle this."

With a quick wave she hurried out the door and down the steps. She was half afraid that her parents were going to follow her to the car and insist that they accompany her and Alex to child care services and it was all she could do not to look over her shoulder to see if they were emerging from the house. But as she strapped Bowie and his carrier into the back seat of her small car, the front door remained closed and Sierra drove away with a sigh of relief.

"Yesterday you chased a potential client out of the office and today you tell me to cancel your last two appointments." Pauline tsk-tsked her tongue as she paced back and forth in front of Alex's desk. "I really want you to see a doctor, hon. As far as I can tell, you're cracking up."

Alex, who'd been trying to concentrate on the notes he'd made during the trial this morning, snapped his head up with irritation.

"Damn it, Pauline, don't you have anything better to do than to make noise in my office? Go make some coffee or file your nails. God knows you're not going to do any work around here anyway."

Pauline stopped in front of Alex's desk and folded her arms across her chest. "And you are?" she asked in an incredulous tone. "Tell that to the two people who wanted to discuss their problems with you *today*. Not tomorrow or the next day."

Tossing down his pencil, Alex glared at her. "Pauline, one of these days that nose of yours is going to get you into deep trouble. It's none of your business why I'm taking the rest of the afternoon off."

She pooh-poohed his sarcasm. "Well, you're so right, Counselor. Your secretary and general right-hand woman doesn't need to know what her boss is up to. If anyone calls I can just wing it and say you're out meeting with a go-go dancer who forgot to keep her clothes on."

Leaning back in his chair, Alex ran a hand over his hair as he thoughtfully studied his secretary. "You really want to know where I'm going?" he asked after a moment.

"Is Texas big?"

A clever grin spread across his face. "I'm going to the offices of child care services."

His secretary was clearly disappointed. "Oh. I thought you had some wild, hot afternoon date or something," she confessed, then frowned in puzzlement. "I don't know of anyone who's been in the office that's needed your help with child services. I—"

Pauline's words broke off as the tinkling sound of the outer door of the building was opened and closed.

"Well, what do you think about that?" she whispered toward Alex. "I might get to go to work, after all."

Alex chuckled as he watched his secretary scurry out of his office. It was just about time for Sierra to be showing up with little Bowie. Pauline was definitely going to be surprised to see the both of them. And no doubt his clever secretary would take one quick look at the baby and know that Sierra was the woman who needed him.

Tucking away his legal notes, Alex rose from his chair and carried the manila folder over to a tall file cabinet.

As he slipped the notes into the proper spot, Sierra's voice sounded behind him.

"Am I interrupting?"

Alex turned and was instantly jolted by the sight of his sweet friend. She was dressed in a close-fitting beige sheath and matching high heels. The color enhanced her rosy-tan skin and made her black hair even blacker. This afternoon she had the mass of curls pinned up on the back of her head with a few stray coils left to dangle against her neck. She looked sexy and sophisticated at the same time. And, like an idiot, he wondered if she'd dressed up for his sake or only to make an impression at child care services.

Whistling under his breath, Alex walked over to her. "My, my, you look—fabulous."

His compliment brought a bright blush of pink to Sierra's cheeks. "I wanted to make a good impression with child care services," she said.

For some reason, her admission stabbed him with disappointment but he made a point to push the feeling aside. Sierra was just a friend. Her concerns were for Bowie, not him.

"Well, I don't think you'll have any problem doing that," he said. "Where's Bowie?"

"Pauline took one look at him and snatched him from me."

Slipping his arm around Sierra's waist, Alex urged her toward the door. "We'd better get in there before she ruins him."

"Alex!" Pauline scolded as Alex and Sierra entered the outer office. "You didn't tell me that Sierra was the guardian of a new baby!"

"I haven't had time. And she's not yet officially the guardian. That's why we're headed to child care services," Alex told her.

Pauline turned a coy look on her boss. "Oh. Sierra's your reason for time off. I now forgive you."

"What did she mean by that?" Sierra asked as she and the baby and Alex left the law office.

Alex made a dismissive shrug of one shoulder. "Pauline was cranky with me because I changed some appointment dates."

"Oh, Alex, I didn't want to interrupt your work," Sierra said with regret. "I hope none of this causes you any problems."

"Forget it, Sierra. Court appearances are always being changed from one day to the next so I'm always juggling appointments. It's no big deal."

Alex's black SUV was parked behind the building, forcing them to walk down the block and then cut through to a back alleyway. Alex carried the baby while giving Sierra a steadying hand over the rough asphalt of the back street.

Once they reached the SUV, he buckled the baby in the back seat, then helped Sierra into the front bucket seat before he took his place behind the wheel. Although she'd taken short trips around town with him before, being enclosed in such a small space with him now somehow felt different to Sierra. She tried to hide her nervousness as she glanced over at him and smiled.

Oh my, oh my, she thought. Why was she suddenly seeing a sexy, intelligent lawyer instead of an old college pal? Why was she charmed by the loop of brown hair falling onto his forehead and the dimple that was coming and going in his cheek? This was Alex. Her old friend, Alex. She wasn't supposed to be noticing him like this.

"Uh—I took the baby by my parents just before I drove to your office," Sierra said, hoping a little conversation would get that marble in her brain back in the right spot. "They were—surprised, to say the least. I'm not so sure they think it's a good idea for me to keep Bowie. But that doesn't surprise me," she added wryly.

Alex glanced at her as he wheeled them into the flow of traffic. "Why do you say that? Your parents have always seemed like very understanding people to me."

Sierra twisted her hands together in her lap. "They are. But I'm their youngest child. They don't think I'm grown up enough to do anything so serious as take on the responsibility of a baby."

Alex's brows lifted and fell in contemplation. "Well, it is a serious thing. But you're not an idiot." He slanted her a sardonic glance. "You're only one of those when it comes to choosing boyfriends."

"Gee, Alex, how sweet of you to say so."

Laughing at her retort, he reached over and picked up one of her hands. Sierra nearly gasped out loud as he lifted the back of her hand to his lips.

"I can't get over how gorgeous you look today. I didn't know you had it in you," he teased.

And she never knew that a compliment from Alex could make her feel so feminine or desirable. Through the years, Sierra had always seen herself as lacking in the looks department. Especially when she compared herself to her glamorous sisters. To have a man of the town like Alex imply that she was gorgeous was enough to set her heart to pounding.

"Alex, you don't have to spread it on. I'm feeling confident about this afternoon."

Alex's gaze slid discreetly over her crossed legs. Although she was a petite woman, she was shaped like an hourglass. Even her legs were curvy and smooth, the kind that called for a man to touch and slide his hand against them.

While his covert glance traveled from her calf down to her ankle, he surprised himself by wondering what she would do or think if he were to reach over and place his hand on her knee. The fine-gauged material of her stockings would gently rasp against his fingertips. The warmth of her body would seep into his palm.

"Alex! Didn't you hear me, or are you off in some courtroom?"

Jerking his wayward thoughts back to the present, he glanced at her and hoped he wasn't blushing. She might not find his erotic thoughts too funny. Sierra wasn't a prude, but she abhorred sleaziness.

"Uh—sorry, I was just thinking about something. What did you say?"

"I asked if you'd talked to your parents. If you'd told them about Bowie and what you were doing for me."

The slow curl of heat that had been coiling around in Alex's groin suddenly froze. "No. Why would I want to?"

Sierra shrugged before she looked over her shoulder at Bowie. The movement of the car was keeping him sound asleep. His pug little chin was tucked against his chest and hidden beneath the collar of his shirt. His head had drooped to one side and he was sucking intermittently on the pacifier she'd placed in his mouth at the start of the trip. She figured the baby was less than a week old and probably weighed no more than seven or eight pounds. But each time Sierra looked at him, she could easily see a young boy learning to ride a bike, a young man graduating college.

"Why not? They'd be pleased to know that you're helping a child find a home."

"Like they did?" he quipped dryly.

"Alex," she scolded softly as she reached over and placed her hand on his shoulder. "I thought you'd forgiven them for not telling you about your adoption. It's been so long now since you found out about it. Why does it still rile you so?"

He let out a rough sigh as he braked the car at a red light. "It doesn't rile me, Sierra. I just—wish they could have been honest with me."

Regret and a sweet sense of caring filled her as she quietly studied his grim profile. "And would that have made you happy? If they'd started out telling you at a very young age that your mother had deserted you on the steps of a building? I'm not so sure, Alex."

"Let's not talk about this, Sierra," he clipped back at her.

Pressing her lips together, she dropped her hand from his shoulder. She'd always wanted to make Alex see that his being adopted didn't mean he was any less of a man than the next guy. He'd been raised in a normal, loving household. He'd been blessed and he needed to remember those blessings instead of dwelling on the subterfuge of how he'd come to be a part of the Calloway family.

But now was not the time to dig into him about it. She needed his help and when you ruffled his feathers,

Alex was unpredictable. If she made him angry, he just might turn the car around, head back to his office and tell her to deal with Bowie on her own.

"All right, Alex."

The tight grip he had on the steering wheel eased. "Sierra, Bowie will be a man someday and then he—"

Sierra waited patiently for him to finish, but silent moments continued to tick away until she prompted, "Then he what, Alex? What were you going to say?"

Shaking his head, he said, "It wasn't important. And here's the block of Department of Human Services buildings. We're here." He pulled into the nearest parking slot he could find and killed the engine. "Let's go in and get this over with."

Chapter Four

Three days later, on the Mendoza backyard patio, Sierra stood next to her father as he tested a slab of brisket cooking on the barbecue grill. The scent of the juicy beef was enough to make Sierra's mouth water. Her stomach growled hungrily as her father closed the lid.

"Dad, it can't need much more cooking," she protested. "When are you going to take it off the fire?"

With a chuckle, Jose patted his youngest daughter's shoulder. "A little more patience, honey. By the time you help your mother get the rest of the food out here on the picnic table, the brisket will be ready."

Relieved that supper was finally near, Sierra hurried into the house to help her mother gather up the accompanying dishes Maria had prepared earlier in the day.

The two of them were setting everything onto the outdoor table when Gloria and her fiancé, Jack Fortune, emerged from the back door of the house.

"You must have smelled food," Maria said happily at the sight of her middle daughter. "Do you two have time to join us?"

Jack, a tall man with short black hair and blue eyes, sauntered over to his soon-to-be mother-in-law and placed a kiss on her cheek.

"We'll make time, Maria," he said. "Gloria heard through Sierra that Jose was cooking brisket. So we invited ourselves."

Jack was Patrick Fortune's son and nephew to Ryan who owned the Double Crown Ranch just outside Red Rock. Up until about three months ago, the powerful businessman had been living and working in Manhattan. But Patrick had decided to send his son down to San Antonio to help Gloria establish her jewelry business.

To the whole family's surprise, Jack and Gloria had established more than a thriving new business. Their baby was due in early fall and their wedding plans were going at a brisk pace.

"That's good," Jose spoke up from his position at the barbecue grill. "We've got enough food here to feed an army. Does anybody know if Christina is coming?"

"She said that she and Derek would try to make it," Gloria stated as she hugged her mother and then her father. "But she wasn't sure. They've been doing a lot of extra work lately at Fortune-Rockwell Investments."

Sierra put down the handful of utensils she was holding and hurried over to greet her sister. As usual, Gloria was a fashion plate in a pair of white capri pants and a red-and-white striped blouse that tied at the waist and exposed her slightly growing belly. Her light brown hair was twisted into a sexy knot at the back of her head and gold hoops swung from her ears. She was so beautiful it was no surprise that one of San Antonio's most eligible bachelors had fallen for her. Sierra had always felt dowdy in comparison. But her lack in looks wasn't really important to her anymore. Especially now that she had little Bowie. He'd made all of her values take on an entirely different direction.

"Sierra, I'm so glad you're here," Gloria said as she hugged Sierra tightly. "Mom has told me all about the baby. Where is he? I want to see him!"

"That's all she's been talking about," Jack spoke up with a wink. "Maternal hormones at work."

Laughing softly, Sierra took her older sister by the arm and urged her toward a door that would take them into the kitchen. "Bowie's in the house, in my old bedroom. I was just about to go in and get him."

As the two women walked through the kitchen and down a long hallway, Gloria said, "I was so surprised when Mom told me about the baby. I couldn't believe the mother just left him like that. Now that I'm going to marry the man that I love and have his baby, it's made me see my role as a woman in a different light. I don't have to think twice. My child and my husband will always come first in my life."

Sierra glanced at Gloria and couldn't help but feel a

pang of envy. Even though she'd been blessed with little Bowie, he didn't officially belong to her. Child services could take him away at any moment. And with Chad now gone with the wind, there was no chance she'd be having a child of her own anytime soon.

"Gloria, you know how happy I am for you and Christina, too. It was so awful when you were both gone. I tried to fill the void with Mom and Dad as best I could. But I wasn't enough to make up for you and Christina."

Gloria spared her sister a regretful look. "Christina and I made life terrible for you, Sierra. I don't know how either one of us can ever make it up to you."

Sierra quickly shook her head. "Don't be silly. I just want the both of you to be happy."

By now the two women had reached Sierra's old bedroom. The door was ajar and without waiting for her sister's permission Gloria pushed it aside and hurried into the room.

Thankfully, Bowie was already awake and the happy squeal that Gloria emitted when she saw him lying in the middle of the bed didn't do anything but catch his attention.

"What a precious! Sierra, he's gorgeous!"

Unexplained pride surged through Sierra as she watched an enchanted smile spread across Gloria's face as her sister leaned over the baby for a closer inspection.

"Talk about changing your life," Sierra said wryly. "Having a little one in the house makes everything different."

"No late-night dates with Chad, I'll bet," Gloria said. Then, as soon as the comment passed her lips, she slapped a hand over her mouth. "Oh, Sierra, I'm so sorry! I keep forgetting that you and Chad called it quits. I wasn't thinking." Concerned now, she straightened away from the baby to study Sierra. "How are you doing?"

Sierra shrugged. "To tell you the truth, I think I'm better off without Chad Newbern. He wants to play the field. He wants excitement in his life. My wants are more centered on hearth and home. Boring, huh? But that's just me and I can't change for anyone."

Gloria slung her arm around Sierra's slumped shoulders. "There's not one boring thing about you. You're the sweetest sister any girl could have. You stuck up for Christina and me when we were both—well, more than a little misguided." She wrinkled her nose affectionately at Sierra. "And I'll tell you something else, you're going to find someone who'll be a hell of a lot better for you than Chad Newbern."

Collecting a clean diaper off the dresser top, Sierra went over to the bed and began to change Bowie.

"You sound like Alex," Sierra said. "He's been shouting hallelujah at Chad's departure."

Gloria tapped a thoughtful forefinger against her pretty chin. "Mom said Alex signed papers with you so that you could keep Bowie. That was awfully big of him."

The corners of Sierra's lips tilted upward. "Yeah. Alex can be wonderful when he wants to be."

"I'm wondering why he did it. There wasn't anything in it for him," Gloria said, pondering out loud.

Sierra frowned at her sister's remark. "Gloria! Alex isn't one of those unfeeling lawyers who have nothing on their mind but winning a case and making big bucks."

Linking her fingers together, Gloria walked over to the bed and sat down facing her sister. "Really? That surprises me to hear you say that. I always remember you saying he was one of the most callous, unfeeling men you'd ever known."

A rosy color swept across Sierra's high cheeks. "Well, he can be that way," she admitted. "But lately he seems to be changing—mostly for the good."

Gloria's delicately arched brows inched upward. "Mom says he told child services that you two were getting married. What brought that on? Wishful thinking on his part?"

Sierra laughed heartily as she smoothed the sticky tabs on Bowie's clean diaper. "Not hardly! Do you honestly think a man like Alex Calloway would take a second look at me?"

"Of course I do," Gloria answered with conviction. "You're an intelligent, educated woman who has a wonderful gift for dealing with people. On top of all that, you're pretty and sexy. What more could a man ask for?"

Sierra rolled her eyes before she turned a sardonic look on Gloria. "Uh, maybe a sister to feed his ego?"

Gloria laughed. Sierra picked up Bowie and carefully rose to her feet. "Come on. Dad's surely got the brisket off the grill by now."

By the time Sierra drove back to town and turned

onto Austin Street, it was well past dark. She certainly wasn't expecting to find a vehicle parked in her driveway at this late hour.

Was that Alex's SUV? She parked next to the black vehicle and as she climbed out to the ground, she spotted him standing on the porch, leaning lazily against one of the carved post. The unexpected sight of him filled her with a sweet sense of pleasure and she knew her smile could be heard in her voice as she called out to him.

"What are you doing here?"

"Waiting for you." He jumped off the edge of the porch and walked across the short driveway to meet her. "I was just about to give up and go when I saw your headlights. Where's Bowie?"

This was the second time he'd been to her house this week. Alex just didn't call on her like this. Not unless he had some sort of agenda. But for the life of her, she couldn't imagine what that might be, unless he was here just as a way to show a little concern for their new charge.

Sierra motioned toward the car. "In the back seat. Want to get him out for me?"

"Sure." He opened the back door and leaned in to unfasten Bowie from the car carrier. "Where have you been? I've been waiting for ages."

He cradled the baby in the crook of his arm. Sierra collected the diaper bag from the car and the two of them started to the house.

"Why didn't you call first?" she questioned. "I drove out to my parents' to have supper."

They stepped up onto the porch and he held the screen door out of the way while she unlocked the main, wooden door.

As Alex followed her into the house, he said, "I took it for granted that you'd be home. I didn't think you'd be out gallivanting around with little Bowie. Especially at this hour."

Sierra laughed with disbelief. "It's only eight o'clock, Alex. And I was hardly gallivanting. You sound like a jealous husband or something," she joked.

Alex grimaced as he gazed down at Bowie. He supposed he was getting close to sounding possessive. And to tell the truth, just before Sierra had shown up, he'd been getting downright annoyed that she wasn't yet home. He'd driven all the way over here because he'd wanted to see her. And he'd wanted to see the baby. Finding them gone had been more disappointing than he wanted to admit.

"All right. Make fun of me. But I've had a hell of a long day in the courtroom and I drove all the way over here just to see how you and Bowie were doing."

The tartness in his voice caught Sierra's attention and she looked at him with surprise. "Well, I'm sorry, Alex," she said contritely. "And I am glad you're here."

He offered her a halfhearted smile. "I'm glad I'm here, too."

"Good. Now that we got that out of the way, would you like something to eat? I brought food home from my parents'. Brisket, potato salad, pinto beans and corn bread."

This time he really smiled at her and she felt that sudden surge of joy rushing up in her like an overflowing fountain. What in the world was going on with her anyway? she wondered. It wasn't like her to get a bubbly feeling around a man. And especially not Alex. If he knew some of the things she'd been thinking about him lately, he'd have a fit. And she'd be rightly embarrassed.

"You little darlin'," he crooned. "How did you guess I was starving?"

"You have the look of a hungry man," she said with a knowing smile. "Just have a seat and I'll go carry in the food from the car."

Sierra's mother had placed all the covered containers of food into one large cardboard box to make it easier for Sierra to transport into her car. Sierra carried in the load and quickly set about placing everything onto the table.

When she returned to the living room to announce that the meal was ready, she found Alex sitting on the couch with Bowie still cradled in his arms. He was talking to the baby about selecting jurors and how important it was to look into a person's eyes to gauge their honesty. Bowie appeared to be mesmerized by the legal lesson and, just as Sierra approached the two of them, he gave Alex a toothless smile.

"Look at this, Sierra," Alex said excitedly. "He's smiling at me! I'll bet he's never done that to you!"

Only two dozen or more times, but Sierra wasn't about to burst Alex's proud bubble. It was nice—no, it was more than nice—to have him wanting to be something special to the baby.

"Nope. He must really be impressed with all that law jargon," Sierra told him.

"He should be. It took years of having my nose stuck in a book to get it." He glanced up at Sierra. "Supper ready?"

She nodded. "I'll push Bowie's bassinet into the kitchen and he can lay in it while you eat."

The old house had a big, roomy kitchen with high ceilings and a row of windows that looked onto a back porch that was shaded by a huge pecan tree. Beneath the windows was an old white farm table covered with a red tablecloth. In the middle she'd lit a hurricane lamp just to make the room a bit cozier.

Why Sierra had wanted to make things cozy was beyond her. She wasn't about to set her eye on any man. Like her sisters, she'd sworn off men. Yeah, and look at her sisters now, she thought wryly. Their lives now centered around a special man. But that didn't mean that Sierra was going to succumb to the opposite sex. No, this last experience with Chad had left her feeling like a complete idiot. She didn't want to repeat the process. Even with someone as handsome as Alex.

The two of them carefully situated Bowie in the bassinet and then took their seats kitty-cornered to each other at the breakfast table. While Alex dug into the food, Sierra sipped on a glass of iced tea.

"You'll have to overlook the mismatched dishes," she apologized. "They're some of the restaurant's throwaways. When I moved into this old house, Mom wanted to buy me a new set of dishes, but I discouraged her from that. The odds and ends match me better."

"Who cares about matching dishes," Alex said just before he bit into a forkful of tender smoked brisket. "Mmm. No wonder Red is so popular. Your parents are the best cooks in the world."

"They are," Sierra agreed with a proud smile. "But it's been years since they've actually done any of the cooking in the restaurant. Thankfully it was successful enough for them to hire cooks and all the help they needed to make it run smoothly. Now they're coasting on easy street."

She watched him eat for a moment, then asked, "Why were you in court late today? Trouble?"

He shook his head as he chewed. "Not really. Just arguing a motion to suppress evidence."

Propping her chin on her fist, she studied him with interest. "How did the judge rule? In your favor?"

"I wish," he answered, then frowned. "She won't make a ruling until next week. The trial will resume after that."

"Oh." Lifting her chin, she leaned her shoulders against the back of the chair. For some reason she was finding it hard to relax. Her gaze kept wandering over the navy blue pin-striped shirt Alex was wearing. The fabric accentuated his broad shoulders and the rolled-back cuffs exposed strong forearms sprinkled with dark hair. Sometimes she'd heard him talking about working out at the gym and it definitely showed in the hard, muscular shape of his body.

His body is off-limits to you, Sierra. Don't even think about it.

"So what did Pauline think about Bowie?" she asked as she struggled to get her mind on safer topics.

"What does any woman think about a baby when she sees one?" he asked flippantly. "She oohed and aahed and then she wondered what in heck I was doing getting tangled up in such a mess."

"I beg your pardon! Bowie is not a mess," she said with a huff that told him she was clearly insulted.

Alex waved his fork at her. "She didn't say he was. At least she didn't use the word "mess." But she implied that she thinks Bowie's parentage could come into question and there won't be anything either of us will be able to do about it."

Uneasy now, Sierra leaned anxiously toward him. "I don't know why there should be a problem. If called upon, I'm sure Ginger would sign her rights to the baby over to me. She hasn't shown up here these past few days and I'd bet my last dollar that she isn't going to."

Alex's fork paused in midair, as he looked over at her. "Pauline doesn't understand why I've gotten involved. And, frankly, I don't, either."

Suddenly, keeping Bowie meant nothing without Alex along.

Reaching over, she gripped his hand with hers. "Are you regretting signing those papers with me?" she asked bluntly.

Was he? Over the past week Alex had asked himself that same question several times and all it had taken for an answer was to think about the joy on Sierra's face when she held Bowie to know that he'd done the right thing.

"Are you?" he countered.

"Never," she uttered passionately.

A brief smile crossed his face. "Then I don't regret it, either."

A long sigh of relief eased from her lungs. "I saw Gloria this evening at my parents'. She and Jack had supper with us. Being pregnant herself, she was enamored with Bowie."

Alex glanced over at the baby. "Hmm. You're enamored with Bowie and you're not pregnant. Or are you?" he said teasingly.

Sierra's mouth popped open. "Alex! Do you always have to be—such a lawyer!"

Actually it wasn't the lawyer in him that had prompted the question. As a man and as a friend, he wanted to know.

With a nonchalant shrug, he said, "Well, you appeared to be crazy about Chad 'the loser.' And you were so torn up when he left that I was thinking—something more than just breaking up was bothering you."

Rising to her feet, she went over to the sink and, turning her back to him, began to rinse a few glasses she'd used earlier in the day. "Not that torn up," she muttered. "And there's not a chance I'm pregnant."

Alex's brows lifted slightly as he studied her rigid posture. "You sound awfully positive. Weren't you and Chad that close?"

Incredulous that he was probing into her love life, Sierra turned and folded her arms against her breasts as she faced him. "Do you really think what I did or didn't do with Chad is any of your business?"

A crafty grin teased his lips. "Probably not. But I am the foster father of your child. That ought to garner me some privileges," he argued.

Slapping her hand against her forehead, she shook her head in dismay. How could she be irked at the man when he was sitting there looking so adorable with his collar open, his sleeves rolled up, his brown hair rumpled and the dimples in his cheeks aimed straight at her?

"Oh, I suppose it does," she conceded, trying her best to sound cross with him but failing terribly. "So for your information, Chad and I weren't lovers."

He didn't appear to be all that surprised by her confession. In fact, he almost seemed pleased about the news. Or maybe that was just amusement on his face, Sierra thought.

"Why not?" he asked.

Wiping her hands against the front of her jeans, Sierra walked back over to the table and sank onto the seat she'd occupied before he'd begun cross-examining her.

"I just wasn't quite sure I wanted to take that big of a step with him," she admitted. "Now I'm glad I didn't."

Alex's gaze suddenly took on a new light as he probed her pretty face. "Don't tell me you're still a virgin."

Hot color poured into her cheeks. "Believe me, I won't tell you that," she snapped back at him. "My innocence, or lack of it, is none of your business. Besides, being a virgin is nothing to be ashamed of."

Surprised to see her punching back at him, he countered smoothly, "I didn't say it was." Then, pushing his empty plate back, he glanced over at the counter. "Got any coffee made?"

At least his blatant hint got them off the subject of her love life and she gladly rose to her feet and started gathering the makings for a pot of coffee. "It doesn't take you long to make yourself at home, does it?"

"No. Sorry. But you have a way of doing that to me, Sierra," Alex said as he watched her graceful movements.

He didn't go on to tell her that she was the only woman he'd ever felt completely comfortable with, the only one who made him want to kick off his shoes and lay down on her couch.

If he allowed himself to really think about things, he'd have to admit that he was here tonight because being with Sierra made him feel good. She had always made him feel good. And his lonely apartment did nothing to nurture a cynical soul.

With a fatalistic sigh, he rose to his feet and walked over to her. As he placed his hand against her back, her head twisted around and up. Her brown eyes were wide, her soft, pink lips slightly parted and the sudden realization that he desperately wanted to kiss her hit him like the wham of a baseball bat.

"Is something wrong?" she asked as she spotted the tiny frown marring his forehead.

"I—er, no. Not a thing," he said. Then, taking her by the upper arms, he moved her aside and reached for the glass carafe. "Let me finish making the coffee, honey. You've already done enough for me tonight."

Chapter Five

By the time the coffee had dripped, Bowie had fallen asleep. Alex pushed the bassinet onto the back porch. Sierra followed with the coffee and two bowls of dewberry cobbler.

A soft south wind was blowing in from the gulf, warming the already humid air. Frogs and insects were singing a nighttime lullaby and far across the yard a whip-poor-will's cry pierced the steady chorus.

"He must be lost," Alex commented about the night bird. "I haven't heard one of those around here in ages."

"I hope he stays," Sierra said as she took a seat next to Alex on the porch swing. "He'll eat the mosquitoes."

She hadn't been all that keen on coming outside with him tonight. Not that she disapproved of being outdoors. Truth was she loved being out here. Many of her sleepless nights were spent here on this back porch. But where Alex was concerned, these past few days she'd been having strange vibrations around him. The closer she got to him, the more awkward she felt. And sitting next to him like this in the dark wasn't helping the matter one whit.

"You think Bowie will be all right? We don't want a mosquito to get on him," Alex said between bites of cobbler.

"The netting I draped over him will keep him in fine shape. And I've already discovered that he loves it outside. Isn't it amazing how such a tiny baby could know when he's out of doors?"

"You're learning a lot about babies since you got Bowie, aren't you?"

He'd pushed the swing into a lazy sway and Sierra found the movement made her think of slow, hot hands and hard, warm lips.

"Yes."

He put down his spoon for a moment. "You talked about seeing Gloria tonight. Are you jealous that she's marrying into the rich Fortune family? And that Christina is engaged to a highly successful businessman?"

If anyone else had asked her such questions she would have been offended, but Alex was a lawyer, he couldn't help himself. And he didn't really poke and prod as a way to hurt her.

"No. I'm very happy for both of them. You know me, Alex. Money never was my main agenda or I certainly wouldn't have gone into social work." She waved her hand around her. "You can see how modestly I live. And that's the way I like it. Gloria and Christina are different. Not that either of them are money hungry, but they do live lifestyles that are nothing like mine."

"But Gloria is pregnant. She's going to give your parents their first grandchild. They're fawning over her when you're the one who stuck by Marie and Jose while their two older daughters were off, refusing to come home for even a brief visit."

Sierra thoughtfully pushed the cobbler around her bowl. "There are times I can't help resenting the way both of them behaved—the seemingly careless way they hurt my parents by leaving the family."

"You were hurt, too," Alex said softly. "You don't think I've forgotten all the pain and heartache you went through when you tried to patch the broken relationship between your two sisters, do you?"

To be honest, she was surprised he remembered anything about her personal life. He'd always seemed bored or annoyed with her family sob stories. This past year, whenever her group of friends had met at the Longhorn, she'd tried her best to keep her contribution to the conversation away from her personal life just because she couldn't take Alex's disdain. And she'd done a pretty good job of it, until a couple months ago when she'd announced to her friends that Chad had flown the coop.

"I wasn't sure you remembered any of that time," she admitted.

"Sierra," he scolded gently. "You must think I'm a

real monster. Of course I remember it. I hated all those damn tears you cried."

"Well, I'm not crying them anymore. And I'm very happy that Gloria is going to have a baby. I might be a little envious, but I'll have my turn someday. And besides, I have Bowie and he already feels like my very own," she said softly.

He didn't say anything to that and Sierra finished the last few bites of her dessert before she looked over at him.

"What's the matter?" she asked. "You're silently laughing because you think I'll never find a man who'd put up with me on a permanent basis?"

Alex shook his head. "No. I wasn't thinking anything of the sort. I was wondering—how long do you plan on keeping Bowie as your foster child?"

Her gaze flew to the bassinet sitting a few steps away from them. It was impossible to imagine not having Bowie with her. It was unbearable to envision a life where she couldn't see him take his first step or say his first word. She needed to be there when he started school, when he began to play sports and date girls. She realized she was getting beyond herself, but her heart was moving far faster than the realistic hopes in her head.

"I don't know, Alex. I've been thinking a lot about some of the things you said. And you're right."

He placed his empty bowl on the porch floor and stretched his long legs out in front of him. "Hmm. Something is wrong for you to be agreeing with me."

She ignored his flip remark. "Bowie needs more than just what I can give him. He needs a father, too. And I want him to have the very best. I don't want him to miss out on anything in life. But—" she halted as her throat tightened painfully "—I don't want to give him up. I've got to keep him, Alex, at least for a little while longer."

Turning on the seat, he took hold of both her hands. As he squeezed her fingers, Sierra sniffed to ward off the tears threatening to spill onto her cheeks. The last thing she wanted Alex to think was that she was a sniveling little girl who still had a lot of growing up to do.

"You're getting attached to him," he stated.

Nameless emotions squeezed her heart. "I believe you're getting attached to him, too, Alex."

He shifted closer as his green eyes wandered over her face. "Yeah, I guess I am," he admitted after a moment. "But that's not what's worrying me."

Sierra's heart began to thump harder and faster. His face was getting so close to hers that she could see the pores in his skin, smell the masculine cologne clinging to his clothes. Heat radiated from his body and seemed to arc into her like a hot beam of light. Her breath lodged in her throat and though she kept telling herself to pull back from him she felt her head tilting forward.

"What's worrying you?" she asked in a raspy whisper.

"What to do about this," he murmured.

Sierra was given no time to ask about "this." In fact, she didn't even have time to suck in a shocked breath before she saw Alex's face drawing closer and felt his lips touching hers.

A tiny moan of disbelief sounded in her throat and fearing she was going to pull away from him, Alex framed her face with both hands and held her head gently but firmly as he explored the soft, full curves of her lips.

The taste of her was sweet, delicious and, oh, so precious. Alex had never expected kissing her to feel so warm and wonderful and he realized with a shocked start that he wanted the kiss to go on and on. He wanted to deepen the union of their lips and crush her body up against his.

A need for air was finally the thing that caused Alex to lift his head and stare at her in stunned silence.

Sierra pressed her fingertips to her swollen lips and stared back.

"What was that?" she finally managed to ask.

He swallowed as a strange sort of exhilaration rushed to his head and whirled his senses about like a sudden tornado.

"If I have to explain, then you're way more innocent than I ever thought."

Jumping to her feet, she scurried over to the bassinet, then turned and tossed her hair out of her face before she locked gazes with him. "I know what it was! I mean—why? Why did you kiss me?"

Feeling stupid, but happy, Alex held his palms up in a helpless gesture. "Because I'd been wanting to kiss you all evening."

His honesty floored her and she realized her knees had turned to two pieces of sponge. But whether that malady was from his words or his kiss, she wasn't quite sure.

"Alex! We're—we're friends," she sputtered.

Pushing himself up from the swing, he closed the

short distance between them and placed his hands on her shoulders. Beneath his fingers, he could feel her trembling and he wondered if she'd been as besotted with their kiss as he'd been.

"Friends are allowed to kiss," he softly reasoned.

"Not like that."

Her voice was strained and as she turned her face to one side, her expression looked like someone who'd just committed a horrible sin. Alex would have laughed if he hadn't been so scared himself. He didn't know what was happening to him or to Sierra, but each minute he spent with her, he'd felt a tension growing between them. He could no longer simply think of her as his sweet buddy with a heart too big for her own good. Something had opened his eyes to the fact that she was a woman and that she wasn't quite the pushover he'd always thought her to be.

If someone tried to take Bowie from her, Alex knew she'd fight him or her to the bitter end. And if she loved a man, would she fight just as hard for him? She'd allowed Chad to walk away and that could only mean one thing. She hadn't really loved the guy. The notion curled the corners of Alex's lips with a satisfied smile.

"Why not? You have to be friends before you can be lovers."

Her face jerked back to his and their gazes clashed like swords clanging in the darkness.

Lifting her chin to a challenging angle, she protested

in a husky whisper, "We—uh—we aren't going to become lovers!"

The smile on Alex's face deepened to a cocky grin. "You think not, do you?"

She swallowed as the rapid beat of her heart fluttered in her throat like a trapped bird. "I *know* not!"

The words floated out on a gasp, but her shocked reaction didn't deter Alex at all. His hands slid up and down the slope of her shoulders in a slow, sensuous fashion until they finally curled around her throat and his thumbs rested beneath the angle of her jaw.

"You sound awfully sure of that."

And he sounded so all-fired cocksure of himself that needles of fear jabbed her from every direction. She'd not known Alex for years without learning that he usually got what he went after. She just couldn't understand why he suddenly wanted her.

"I am!" she shot back at him. "You're a great friend, Alex. But I, well, having you in my bed is another matter."

His thumbs reached out and rubbed the soft skin of her chin. It was all she could do to keep from shivering with longing.

"It sure is," he suggested in a low, provocative tone.

"You're heartless. You're cocky and infuriating. You're a—a smart-assed lawyer!" She ended with a toss of her head.

"I promise I don't take any of those traits to bed with me. I leave them on the dresser with my wristwatch and billfold."

The image of Alex, tall, tanned and muscular and shedding his clothes for bed, popped into her brain like a tease from an erotic movie trailer.

Groaning, Sierra twisted loose from his grasp and reached for Bowie's bassinet.

"Please, open the door. I'm taking Bowie back inside. And you're leaving," she said primly.

"Leaving! I haven't even finished my coffee," he complained.

"I'm sure you can make yourself another pot when you get home," she said as she started pushing the bassinet toward the door.

Home. He'd never thought of that damned apartment as home. He was a bachelor. He'd never wanted a home for himself or even thought of what one might be like. Meals on the table and a pretty little wife hovering over him had never been on Alex's agenda. But tonight, this old house seemed like a place where he wanted to stay and he wanted Sierra to do far more than hover over him.

"All right," he said crossly. "I'll leave. But if you think we can just go back to being old college buddies, you're out of your mind."

With that he opened the door and helped her push Bowie and the bassinet back inside the kitchen. Once there, Sierra hurried on to the living room with Alex practically stomping on her heels.

"I was out of my mind all right," she muttered tightly. "For kissing you like I did."

Exasperation twisted his features as he looked at her. "Well, it sure as hell didn't feel like a friendly kiss."

Pushing the bassinet to a stop near the couch, she pulled off the gauze she'd draped over the baby and tossed it to one side. Without looking at Alex, she said, "You've always told me I have poor judgment in men. So I'm taking your advice and not making another mistake with you!"

As Alex headed toward the door, he felt sure his ears were blowing smoke and fire.

"Mistake! For the first time in your life you let yourself act like a woman instead of a—a caretaker! And you call that a mistake! I'm outta here."

Sierra flinched as the door slammed behind him and then, covering her face with both hands, she sank onto the couch. Her whole body was trembling and she was having trouble sucking air into her lungs and pushing it out. Relief didn't come until tears started rolling down her face.

The next morning, Sierra was still in bed when she heard someone pounding on the front door.

With a groggy groan, she jerked on a long cotton robe and stumbled through the living room.

"Who is it?" she called through the door as she swiped her tangled hair out of her face.

"Your sister. Christina."

Oh, thank God, she thought. For a second, she'd feared it might be Alex and she certainly wasn't up to facing him this morning.

Fumbling with the lock, she finally managed to open the door and usher her sister into the house.

At thirty-two Christina was the eldest of the three Mendoza sisters. She was also extremely elegant with a tall, willowy figure and straight, dark brown hair that swung against her shoulders. She was a highly intelligent businesswoman and her job at Fortune-Rockwell had led her straight to the love of her life, Derek Rockwell.

"What are you doing out so early?" Sierra asked as the two of them moved into the living room. Christina and Derek had finally shown up at her parents' barbecue, but thankfully the food was still out on the table, and everyone had been glad to see them in spite of the late hour. "We just saw each other last night at Mom and Dad's."

Christina held up a white bag stamped with a local bakery's logo. The smell of fresh pastries verified that her sister had experienced a sudden breakdown and had stopped to appease her sweet tooth.

"With Gloria and Jack there, I didn't get to talk to you all that much. And I thought you might like to share an apple fritter with me. There's also a cinnamon roll and a chocolate éclair."

Sierra glanced at her sister, who was dressed in a pin-striped suit, and managed to look both professional and beautiful at the same time.

"Dear Lord, you must really be craving sugar this morning," Sierra exclaimed.

"I've got a busy day ahead of me. I need the extra energy," she said as she glanced toward the kitchen. "Got any coffee made?"

Shaking her head, Sierra motioned for Christina to

follow her into the kitchen. "No. I was still in bed when I heard you knocking."

Christina placed the sack of pastries on the kitchen table and turned to study Sierra as she began to spoon coffee grounds into a filter.

"Wow. That's not like you to lie around in bed until seven-thirty. What's wrong? One of your sleepless nights again?"

Sierra nodded. For years now she'd had trouble sleeping. Her busy mind often refused to shut down and last night it had been working overtime. But unlike other nights when her sleeplessness had been caused by work or family matters, this time the cause had been Alex, and Alex only.

"Yeah. I think I finally fell asleep about five o'clock this morning. And then Bowie woke up and let me know he wanted his bottle. By the time I finished feeding him and putting him back to bed I was so exhausted I fell back to sleep."

Christina made an apologetic face at her sister. "Sorry, hon. If I'd known it had been one of those nights, I wouldn't have stopped and woken you. You really should see a doctor about your insomnia, Sierra. It isn't good for your health."

"Christina! Have you forgotten all those doctors that Mom dragged me to when I was in high school?"

"Pooh," Christina scoffed with a dismissive wave of her hand. "That was years ago. You need to try another doctor. Techniques and medicine have probably advanced a lot since you tried to get help."

"I have an update for you," Sierra told her. "I saw one while you and Gloria were living away. All he did was give me sleeping pills and the next morning I woke up so groggy it took me half a day to actually feel energized." With a shake of her head, she dumped cold water into the coffeemaker. "I'll just deal with the problem myself. Besides, last night I just had a lot of things on my mind."

"The baby?"

Christina and Derek had stopped by their parents' house yesterday evening while Sierra and Bowie were still there. Christina had pronounced Bowie adorable, yet Sierra had sensed a lack of enthusiasm in her sister's reaction to the baby. But then Christina had always been the most reserved of the family.

Glancing over her shoulder, she saw a grim look lining Christina's lovely features. It made Sierra wonder what was really going on in her sister's head.

"No. Well, I do think about him a lot," Sierra admitted. "I guess it's pretty obvious that I'm getting attached to the little guy. But I don't know any woman alive who could hold a baby in her arms and hang on to her heart at the same time."

She switched on the coffeemaker and then realizing she'd not cleaned up Alex's supper mess last night, she hurriedly began to pick up the dirty dishes from the table and toss them into the sink.

Christina eased down onto one of the chairs. "I thought you ate at Mom and Dad's last night. What did you do, come home and eat again?" she asked as she surveyed the last of the clutter.

Trying not to appear flustered, Sierra picked up a bottle of Tabasco and stored it in the cabinet. "Uh—Alex came by and I fed him some of the leftovers. Sorry about the mess," she quickly apologized.

"Forget that." She patted the tabletop. "Come on and sit down with me."

"The coffee. It's almost finished dripping."

Christina frowned and pointed to one of the chairs. "Sit. I'll get our coffee in a minute."

Retying the sash of her robe, Sierra took a seat and used her hands to try to calm the riot of black curls falling into her face. "Okay. Here I am."

"Good. It's about time you realized that it's okay to let someone wait on you once in a while, instead of you jumping to everyone else's beck and call."

Leaning back in her chair, Sierra placed a hand against her forehead and feigned a haughty pose. "Yes, I do deserve to be treated like a princess," she joked.

Christina didn't laugh. "You do deserve to be treated like a princess and the sooner you realize that the better."

A puzzled expression crossed Sierra's face. "Did you stop by here this morning to give me a lecture of some sort?"

Glancing over her shoulder, Christina saw that the coffee was finished brewing. She rose to her feet and fetched cups from the cabinet. As she poured the brew, she said, "Not exactly. But I will admit that I'm a little worried about you, Sierra. First you go through that awful breakup with Chad—"

"I'm glad about that. It saved me from discovering what a jerk he was later on."

"Okay. So maybe that was a blessing in disguise," Christina agreed. "But the baby. Frankly, I'm worried about you, hon."

Sierra watched her older sister place the filled mugs and paper plates on the table. A look of concern marred her face and Sierra bristled at the idea that Christina had come swishing in here as though she knew best and it was *her* duty to make sure Sierra walked the right path.

Mentally counting to ten, she shrugged a shoulder. "What's there to be worried about? I'm taking care of a baby. That's all."

Christina eased down into one of the chairs and reached for the bag of pastries. As she handed the apple fritter to Sierra, she said, "And how long do you plan on caring for him?"

Sierra's brows peaked at Christina's pointed question. "Since I've only had him for a few days, it's too early for me to make such a decision."

Christina pulled another pastry from the bag and took a quick bite. "And how do you think you'll feel a week from now? Two weeks from now? As time goes on, don't you think you're going to become even more attached to him?"

"Most normal persons would," Sierra retorted.

Ignoring the waspish tone in Sierra's voice, Christina said, "That's right. And as far as I can see, you're normal. No, scratch that. You're not normal. Your heart is bigger than your head. You've probably already fallen head over heels in love with the cute little guy."

Sierra crammed a piece of the fritter into her mouth. "So what if I have?" she asked between chews. "He needs someone to love him."

Tilting her face toward the ceiling, Christina shook her head. "Oh, my darling sister, don't you see? Loving Bowie would be wonderful if you intended to keep him as your own. But we both know that's impossible and—"

"Why is it impossible?" Sierra interrupted.

A tender look of regret filled Christina's face as she reached over and tucked Sierra's wayward hair back behind her shoulder. "Child services wants to place the baby in a home with two parents. And with Chad gone, I don't see you getting married anytime soon."

Rising from the table, Sierra carried her coffee cup with her as she walked over to the door leading onto the back porch. With the top of the door being constructed of paned glass, it allowed a wide view of the shaded yard and the portion of the porch where she and Alex had sat on the cedar swing. And kissed.

"You really know how to make a girl feel good, sis," Sierra muttered. "This is just what I need in the morning to get me going for the day ahead."

"Oh, Sierra, don't get mad at me. I don't mean it in a demeaning way. You're going to find your Prince Charming and when you do he'll jump at the chance to make you his wife. But that isn't going to happen just because you have Bowie. And without a husband, I can't see child services allowing you to keep him for very long."

Sierra clamped her lips together. She wanted to tell Christina that she and Gloria weren't the only Mendoza women who could attract a man. She wasn't a doormat for men to walk on.

Squaring her shoulders, she glanced over her shoulder at her well-meaning sister. "I guess Mom didn't tell you. Alex told child services that we were getting married."

The pastry in Christina's hand stopped midway to her mouth. "Alex? Alex Calloway? No! Mom didn't say a thing about it," she said in a quiet, shocked voice. "When did this happen? Why didn't you say something about it last night?"

Sierra knew she should explain the whole story to Christina, but it felt too good to let her sister think that she was loved by a hunky lawyer like Alex.

"I didn't say anything because, well, we haven't set a date or anything. We—uh—we've just now realized how we feel about each other." Maybe that wasn't too much of a fib, Sierra thought. She and Alex had definitely felt something for each other last night when they'd kissed like there was no tomorrow.

A smile sparkled across Christina's face. "Boy, do I feel stupid. Here I was doing all this worrying about my sister and now I learn you do have a plan for yourself and the baby."

Sierra returned her sister's smile with a wobbly one of her own. "Well, I'm trying, sis. But who's to say it will all work out." And that certainly was the truth, she thought.

"None of us have any guarantees, Sierra. But I've got to say I think you're on the right track with Alex. He's the first man you've ever been with who didn't need emotional therapy."

Sierra walked back to the table and sank onto a chair. She felt utterly drained and the day was just starting. "Gee, you make it sound like I picked my boyfriends from the mental hospital."

"Don't be silly," Christina scolded. "They were all just a little too needy. If you know what I mean."

"And you think Alex isn't?" Sierra couldn't help but ask.

Christina's smile turned a bit wicked. "Alex's needs are those of a typical man." She winked at Sierra and laughed suggestively. "But I'm sure you've already figured that out."

Sierra hadn't figured anything out about Alex. She wasn't even sure why he'd suddenly inserted himself into her life. Sure they were friends and had been for years. But last night he'd not been behaving like a friend. And heaven forbid, neither had she.

Clearing her throat, Sierra pushed herself up from the chair. "Stay put and finish your coffee, sis. I think I hear Bowie. If he's awake I'll bring him back to the kitchen so that you can say hello."

Christina glanced at her wristwatch. "I was about to say I've got to leave. But I'll stay long enough to kiss Bowie good morning. Derek needs to learn he's not the only male around here to turn my head," she joked.

Glad that she'd managed to put an end to the subject of Alex, Sierra left the kitchen and hurried to collect the baby.

Chapter Six

Two days after Christina's visit, Sierra, feeling house-bound, decided to go to the market for a few groceries for herself and to restock her supply of baby formula and diapers for Bowie.

That afternoon she was carrying the things in from the car when she heard the phone begin to ring. Since she'd already carried Bowie into the house and placed him in a safe spot on the couch, she forgot about the last of her groceries and ran to pick up the phone.

After a breathless hello, a familiar male voice sounded in her ear.

"Where have you been? I've been calling for the past two hours!"

If she'd thought his question had come from male

passion, she would have scolded him. But since there was concern in his voice she wanted to soothe him.

"I went to the market," she explained. "Bowie was running low on a few things. Especially formula."

"The boy must eat like a horse."

Pride surged through her as she glanced at Bowie. The baby was kicking and waving his legs and arms with obvious enthusiasm. Apparently it felt good to him to be out of the confines of the car seat. "He's growing," she said to Alex. "He needs plenty of nourishment."

"I'm glad you brought that up, Sierra. Since we need our nourishment, too, how about going out to dinner tonight?"

Sierra suddenly gripped the phone. "With you?"

He made a sound of disgust. "No, I'm calling to ask you to have dinner with John Gutierrez."

She frowned. "Who's he?"

Alex groaned. "Damn it, Sierra, how should I know! I just made up the name. I'm asking you to go out with me—for dinner."

Sierra felt herself begin to tremble both inside and out. "You mean, like a date?"

"I don't care what you call it," he said impatiently. "It'll be the two of us eating together. No big deal."

Maybe not to him, Sierra thought. But to her it was a giant deal. She'd been out with Alex before and had even shared a meal with him, but only as a friend. This would be different and they both knew it. Especially after that hot kiss he'd given her the last time they'd been together and then the horrible fight that had followed it.

"I don't want to leave Bowie with—anyone."

"I'm not asking you to. He can come along, too. If he starts bawling too loudly we can always get up from the table and take him outside. Like you see all those other harried parents doing."

Just like they were a married couple with a baby, Sierra thought. The idea caused a wistful sigh to pass her lips.

"All right," she said. "Where are we going? So I'll know what to wear."

A grin laced his voice. "I thought we'd go to Red. Like I said, nobody does food better than the Mendozas. I'll pick you up at seven."

At ten minutes to seven, Sierra was ready and waiting for Alex. As she paced nervously around the living room, she caught her reflection in a mirror hanging on a wall behind the couch.

She'd spent an eternity picking out a skirt and then finding a top that looked decent enough to wear with it. Sierra had never been a clotheshorse like Gloria. And since Sierra's job had never required her to purchase expensive pieces, nearly all of her things were casual.

Tonight she'd decided to wear a gored, red floral skirt. On the left side, the hem angled downward into a sexy point against her calf. Her blouse was a white gauzy material that draped across her breasts and tied at the side of the waist. As for her hair, she'd decided to pin it all up in a curly mass atop her head and leave a few tendrils to hang at her ears and the back of her neck. At least with her hair up, she did look like a grown woman, she decided. Whether that was a sensual grown woman, Sierra could only hope.

Alex arrived promptly at seven and after helping Sierra get Bowie buckled safely in his own little seat, he drove the short distance to downtown Red Rock and parked in the massive lot behind the Mendoza restaurant.

Red was located in a converted hacienda that had once been owned by an influential Spanish family rumored to be related to Santa Ana. Thankfully Jose and Maria had been lucky enough to buy the place at an affordable price before anyone realized it was a historical treasure. The structure had been built with two stories, but her parents had chosen to only use the bottom floor for the restaurant. Part of the top floor had been renovated for office use and the remainder was simply used as storage.

There was a beautiful courtyard inside the square of the building, which featured an old fountain that supplied diners with the soft, musical notes of trickling water. Colored umbrellas shaded pine tables and chairs, which were arranged at odd angles among several tall, Mexican fan trees. Bougainvillea grew at every turn and bloomed vividly in fuchsia, purple and gold.

Sierra had to admit that the courtyard was her favorite dining area at Red, but she figured since they had little Bowie with them, it would be safer to keep him inside. The air had grown very hot and humid this evening and she didn't want the baby getting congested.

Alex insisted on carrying Bowie as they walked around the building to the front entrance. Inside the restaurant, a hostess dressed in a long black skirt and a white gypsy-style blouse greeted Sierra by name, then turned to Alex.

"Right this way, Mr. Calloway," the young woman said with a gesture for them to follow her. "We already have your table ready."

Impressed, Sierra glanced up at Alex. "You made reservations?"

His green eyes twinkled down at her. "Of course. I'm a lawyer. I'm always prepared."

They followed the hostess through the main dining area to one of the smaller rooms, which held only a handful of pine tables and chairs. Like the rest of restaurant, it was decorated in typical hacienda style with plenty of southwestern colored blankets and antiques dating as far back as 1845 when President Polk announced Texas the twenty-eighth state of the Union. Paintings depicting the battles between Texans and Mexicans to free the republic from Santa Ana's rule hung along the dark wooden walls here and in the main dining area. No matter how many times Sierra walked through the door of Red, she was reminded how hard her parents had worked to embellish this place with an atmosphere that all Texans, especially those from Red Rock, would enjoy.

The hostess found a special seat to place Bowie's carrier in and after Alex had secured the baby, he helped Sierra into her chair. As he took the seat angled to her right elbow, a waiter hovered to take their orders for drinks.

At the last minute, Sierra decided to be a little reckless and order a margarita. Since she wasn't much of a social drinker, it only took a small amount of alcohol to go straight to her head. But with Alex already making her head spin, what did a little extra drunkenness hurt? she thought wryly.

"I always forget what a fabulous place this is," Alex commented as the waiter disappeared from the room. His gaze roamed appreciatively around the dimly lit walls then came to rest on her face. "But I never forget your sweet face," he added softly.

Feeling totally out of her depth, Sierra clasped her hands together on her lap and tried not to appear as nervous as she felt. "You've gone through a long line of women in your time, Alex Calloway. How do you keep my face separate from theirs?"

Amusement crinkled the corners of his eyes. "It's hard. But I manage." He made a motion with his hand at their surroundings. "I know you've told me that you love to eat in the courtyard, but with little Bowie, I wasn't sure about getting a table out there."

Sierra was totally surprised by his thoughtfulness. "You were right. It's too hot and muggy to have him out tonight." Propping her chin on the heel of her palm, she looked at him. "I thought you didn't know anything about caring for babies?"

Resting his forearms on the tabletop, he leaned toward her and gave her a wicked wink. "I don't. I'm just letting my common sense show. We lawyers have that, too."

Her hand dropped away from her face as she laughed softly. "What on earth has Pauline been putting in your coffee? A lawyer with common sense? You'd be ruined."

"You're being downright cruel tonight, Sierra," he teased just as the waiter appeared with their drinks.

The young man served Sierra a tall, frozen margarita and Alex a glass of red wine. As he was leaving, Maria walked in and headed straight to their table.

"Mom. I didn't realize you were here at the restaurant tonight. I thought you and Dad were home resting," Sierra said with a bit of surprise.

Maria made a comical face. "Dear daughter, your parents don't need to be in a geriatric home yet. We do still have some life left in us."

"Here, here," Alex said with enthusiasm as he lifted his wineglass toward Sierra's mother. "You look beautiful and vibrant tonight, Mrs. Mendoza."

Clearly flattered by Alex's compliment, Maria smiled at him and for a moment Sierra expected to see her mother pat her hair and bat her eyelashes.

"And it's good to see you, too, Alex," Maria said. "Have you been doing well?"

Alex glanced furtively at Sierra, before he turned his gaze back on Maria. "Very well. Thank you for asking."

Maria moved around the table until she was standing over Bowie's high chair. Her expression softened with tenderness as she gazed down at the sleeping baby. "Jose and I are very grateful to you for helping our Sierra keep Bowie," she said to Alex. "At first we were a bit worried about her decision, but now we can see how happy the baby makes her."

"Yes," Alex replied. "And I think we'd both agree that Sierra deserves a little happiness."

Maria looked up just as Alex reached over and lifted the back of Sierra's hand to his lips.

Dear Lord, what was he trying to do? Sierra wondered as she watched her mother's eyes narrow into shrewd, calculating slits.

"Uh, if you two don't mind, I'd like to take Bowie upstairs. Jose and I are having a little snack and we'd like the chance to have the baby with us for a few minutes. Is that all right with you, Sierra?"

What could she say? Sierra wondered. It would sound silly to object, even though Sierra knew with a measure of certainty that her mother hadn't just casually come downstairs to take Bowie off her hands.

"Of course, Mom. His diaper bag is sitting beneath the high chair. You might want to take it with you. Just in case he wakes and acts hungry."

"Oh, babies are my specialty," she happily crooned as she lifted Bowie and his carrier into her arms. "I know exactly how to take care of them. After all, I had three of my own. And now Gloria is expecting and you have Bowie. Maybe Christina will be next and the house will be full of babies." She tilted her chin to a smug angle. "You know, Rosita isn't the only one around here who can have grandchildren."

Maria waltzed out the door with Bowie and the diaper bag. Sierra turned an amazed look on Alex. "I'm worried, Alex. Mom's taken a hundred-and-eighty-degree turn. She's been warning me not to get too attached to Bowie. Now she's behaving like he's her grandchild! And don't think for one minute that she showed up here at our table just by coincidence. Someone told her we were here and for some reason she decided to take our boy off our hands."

Our boy. The sound of that made Alex smile inside, though he couldn't explain why. The notion of him having a son of his own was scary as hell. Raising a child was serious business. If you didn't do it right, you'd leave scars. He ought to know; he had plenty of them himself.

Through the years those scars had hardened until sometimes he wondered if he could ever feel anything for anybody, including himself. But then Sierra had always been around to scold and prod and shame him until she pricked his conscience and he gave in and tried to show her a softer side of himself. Which, most of the time, was always just an act to make her happy.

But in the past few days Alex had to concede that something had happened to him. Ever since Bowie had come into his life, he'd felt himself changing and looking at things in a totally different light. The baby and Sierra had brought an importance to his life that he'd never experienced before. He was beginning to think that maybe his existence did mean more than just courtroom tactics and getting some joker off the legal hook.

"Who's Rosita?" Alex asked.

Sierra reached for her margarita. "Oh, you've heard me speak of her before, Alex. She's the older lady who works as a housekeeper for Lily and Ryan Fortune out at the Fortune ranch. She's been with them for years and years. Mom has tried to get her to retire, but Rosita won't hear of it. I think she likes working because it keeps her in the thick of the Fortune family happenings. She's a distant cousin to Mom and they've been good friends since they were children. Mom is jealous because Rosita has several grandchildren and she's still waiting."

"Oh, yes, I think I do remember you mentioning Rosita before. She's the one who has the prophetic dreams, isn't she?"

Sierra's low chuckle was full of doubt. "Well, some of them have proved to come true. But her family takes all of her prophecies with a grain of salt."

"Maybe we should get her to tell us our fortunes," Alex suggested. "It might be amusing to hear what we'll be doing a year or two from now."

Shaking her head, Sierra said, "Rosita isn't some sort of gypsy woman reading palms. These intuitions or dreams or whatever they are simply come to her. She doesn't ask for them."

Alex shrugged as he sipped his wine. "That's too bad. It would be nice to know if I'm going to win my next case."

Sierra rolled her eyes. As far as she was concerned she didn't want to see what she and Alex would be doing a year or two from now. Especially with him acting so downright seductive toward her.

She shot him a coy look. "I thought you were always certain of a victory in the courtroom."

Laughing softly, he picked up her hand and kissed her fingers. "Honey, you do know how to feed my ego."

Upstairs, in a room that Maria and Jose had furnished as a living room/office, Jose took pleasure in rocking Bowie in an old wooden office chair. Nearby on a dark green couch, Maria shook her finger at her husband.

"I'm telling you, Jose, there's something going on between the two of them. He was kissing her hand!"

Jose smiled to himself. "So."

Maria rolled her eyes. "Ay! Ay! Ay! Do you go around kissing a woman's hand if she's only a friend?"

Jose glanced up from the baby's angelic face. The moment his wife had discovered that Alex had made a reservation for two tonight, her calculating mind had gone into overdrive. She'd insisted that the two of them have their dinner up here in the office so that she could go downstairs and casually meander through the room where Alex and Sierra would be eating and offer to watch Bowie for them.

"Is that a trick question, woman?" Jose asked.

Maria let out a long, impatient breath. Sometimes men could be so slow, or maybe they weren't actually slow, they just pretended to be, she thought.

"Jose Mendoza, I'm not questioning your fidelity. I'm just saying a man doesn't go around kissing a woman's hand out of friendship. Don't you agree?"

Jose cuddled the baby in the crook of his big arm and

turned his attention to his wife. "Maybe. And maybe Alex is attracted to our little girl. Are you worried that he's going to break her heart?"

Maria thought about her husband's question for a moment before she shook her head. "Not really. I'm more worried that she won't take advantage of his attraction. Alex is just right for Sierra. I've never understood why she hasn't noticed that before."

Jose scowled at his wife as she rose to her feet and began to walk back and forth in front of him. "And what makes you think they're so perfect for each other? They've been friends for years. Don't you think something should have sparked between them before now?" Jose questioned.

Maria paused long enough to glance at her husband and bat a hand through the air. "Pooh! Sierra has always had some sort of boyfriend hanging on her arm. And Alex has been too tied up with his career to fall in love."

Shaking his head, Jose clicked his tongue with disbelief. "Boyfriends. Careers. It takes more than that to keep people from falling in love. And while we're on this subject, you need to forget all about pushing Sierra and Alex together. Let nature take its course."

Comic outrage froze her features. "How can you say that to me? Look what I've done for Gloria and Christina! They're happy—they're both going to be married. That's what I want for Sierra. And besides all that, nature takes too damn long."

Marie picked up a finger sandwich from a tray sitting on the corner of a large oak desk and shook it at

Jose as she went on, "Sierra is twenty-eight. She needs to get a life—a family of her own."

Jose bit back a sigh and tried to answer as patiently as he could. "She will. When the time is right. And if Alex is the man for her, then I'm sure she'll let him hear about it."

Maria was thoughtful for a few moments and then a cunning smile spread across her face as she lifted the sandwich to her lips. "Well, at least we have Bowie with us tonight. The two of them can have a quiet, romantic dinner alone."

"I feel lost without Bowie," Sierra said some minutes later as she and Alex partook of a table full of food. For her main dish, Sierra had ordered one of her favorites, grilled chicken breast stuffed with spinach and topped with queso sauce. Every bite was hot and spicy and she found herself reaching frequently for the margarita to cool her tongue.

"I'm sure you do," Alex replied, "but it's good for you to have a rest. I'm glad your mother made the offer to watch him."

Sierra started to tell him that Maria's kindly gesture had been blatantly deliberate, but she didn't bother. Alex had a strong mind of his own. He saw all sorts of people in the courtroom who were experts at manipulation. He certainly couldn't be swayed one way or the other by a meddling, middle-aged woman hell-bent on marrying off her three daughters.

A half hour later, the two of them had finished their

meal and Alex had related to Sierra several amusing incidents that had happened to him in the courtroom when he'd first started practicing law. The laughter and the alcohol had left her feeling a bit giddy and when he suggested they walk out to the courtyard, she was glad for the opportunity to get some fresh air.

As soon as they stepped outside onto the red-brick paving that formed a small patio beneath the eave of the building, the warm, muggy air wrapped around them like a velvet blanket. The trickling water fountain filled the gardenlike area with soothing music while chattering mockingbirds and the gentle cooing of gray doves added their own special notes to the song.

Alex placed his arm lightly against the back of Sierra's waist and guided her toward one of the empty tables situated in the far corner of the courtyard. The space was partially hidden by a thick oleander dripping with white blossoms.

The moment the two of them stepped behind the bush, Alex tugged her into his arms.

"Alex! What—what are you doing?" she stuttered as her palms instinctively came up against the broad width of his chest.

With his head bending downward, he murmured, "Surely you don't have to ask."

Sierra had never expected him to kiss her here, like this, where people were dining only a few feet away! Actually she'd not expected him to kiss her at all. Maybe that was naïve thinking on her part after the heated exchange they'd shared on the porch swing. But she'd pretty much convinced herself that his attraction for her was just a momentary thing. Something he'd get over quickly, like the three-day measles.

Now, as his lips sealed hers with a slow, seductive search, she realized she'd been very wrong. If anything, the desire she felt on his lips was hungry and reckless and totally shocking to her senses.

Stolen moments turned into risky minutes until finally Sierra's knees began to give way and Alex was so starved for air he was forced to lift his head.

"Alex," she said in a breathless rush. "Have you gone crazy? If someone sees us, they'll complain of indecency!"

Nuzzling his cheek against the curve of her neck, he chuckled softly. "I'm a lawyer, remember. If we get charged I can get us off."

Oh Lord, it was heaven to have him touching her, holding her like this, Sierra thought desperately. How could she resist him, when all she really wanted to do was curl her arms around his neck and hang on for dear life?

"Oh," she said in a thick, drowsy voice. "How would you manage to do that?"

His hands began to move up and down across her back. Heat filled every inch of Sierra's body and burned her face like the hot afternoon sun. Why hadn't she ever felt like this before? Why had it taken Alex to wake up the latent woman inside her?

"Demand a jury trial and make sure it was made up of nearly all men. None of them could blame me for wanting to make love with you."

"Alex," she whispered sweetly, "you're so silly."

He brought his face back around to hers and said in a husky voice, "You know, you're right. I've been very silly all these years not to realize how beautiful you are. Inside and out."

Sierra winced as pain and joy balled together and smacked her right in the middle of her chest. "Don't fib, Alex," she pleaded.

Bringing his forefinger beneath her chin, he lifted her face up to his. "I'm not lying," he insisted.

"Then stop trying to charm me."

He looked amused. "Why? Because you think I'm trying to seduce you? Well, I am."

Desperate to hide how shaken she was by his blunt statement, Sierra turned her back to him and sucked in a shaky breath. "I can't understand why. You can have any woman you want. And you've never wanted me."

His hands curled over the back of her shoulders as he bent his head and spoke softly against her ear. "That's not true. I can't have any woman I want. And I've always wanted you as a friend. Now I happen to want you to be more than a friend."

Sierra closed her eyes as all sorts of wicked images danced through her mind. At least he was being honest, she thought. At least he wasn't trying to pretend he felt love for her. Especially when they both knew it was sex. And sex only.

But even knowing that wasn't enough to damper the longing that was growing, spreading through every inch of Sierra's body. She'd never felt such a sudden, overwhelming desire for any man, and maybe a few days ago she would have been too shy and worried to act upon her feelings. But tonight she was feeling anything but timid.

Turning slowly back around to him, Sierra lifted her face and met the dark, smoky glint in his green eyes.

"I think we'd better get Bowie and go home," she murmured. "Don't you?"

Surprise flickered across his face and then he gave her a slow, crooked smile. "Straight home. Without any stops or U-turns."

Chapter Seven

Minutes later, Alex and Sierra were driving the short distance back to Sierra's two-story. In the back, Bowie was fussing and chewing his fist.

"He must be hungry," Alex suggested. "Isn't that what a baby does to try to tell you that he's hungry?"

Twisting around in her seat as far as the seat belt would allow, Sierra studied the baby's red face and jerky arm movements. "I think so. But he shouldn't be hungry. Mom said he just drank a whole bottle of formula."

When the two of them had gone up to her parents' office to pick up Bowie, they'd both made an issue of wanting to keep the baby longer and that they'd not had nearly enough time to spend with him. Maria had even suggested that she keep Bowie overnight to give Sierra a restful night's sleep. But Sierra wouldn't hear of it. She wasn't quite ready to let her little guy be that far away from her. And besides, she got the feeling that Alex was around because baby Bowie was around. She didn't want to take away his chance to spend more time with the baby.

"That may be the problem," Sierra said as her forehead puckered with worry. "He usually doesn't eat that much at a time. He's probably got a tummy ache."

"When a baby has a stomachache, don't you call that colic?" Alex asked.

Sierra groaned. "Yeah. That and a nightmare."

By the time Alex parked his SUV in front of the house and Sierra lifted Bowie out of his carrier, the baby was squalling at the top of his lungs.

"I'll bring the diaper bag. You take him on into the house," Alex told her as she carefully propped the baby against her shoulder.

Sierra went ahead of him and after turning on a lamp, she sank onto a wooden rocking chair and checked Bowie's diaper. It was clean and dry so she ruled that out as the offending culprit.

Alex appeared and set the diaper bag down on the floor next to the rocker. "I've never heard our boy cry like this. He must be miserable," Alex mused aloud as he gazed down at the baby nestled in the crook of Sierra's arm. "And look how he's drawing his legs up. Must be his stomach. What do you do for colic? Is there some sort of medicine you can give him?"

Ashamed that she didn't have answers for all his questions, she said, "I'm sorry, Alex. I've never been a mother before. I'm just learning about all this stuff. Maybe we could call the all-night drugstore and ask the pharmacist?"

"Good idea," Alex said. "I'll call while you see if you can quiet him."

Sierra began to rock and the lulling motion settled his screams to hiccupping wails. Smoothing her fingers over his head, she began to sing a lullaby in hopes her voice would distract him.

Across the room, Alex hung up the phone and hurried back to Sierra and the baby. "He said it sounds like colic and there's not much you can do for it. If he doesn't get better soon, he suggested giving him a few drops of liquid simethicone. But he said before we resort to that, we might try making him burp the gas off his stomach."

Sierra was incredulous. "Use medicine as the last resort? Wouldn't easing his stomach with medicine be better than him screaming with pain?"

Alex shook his head. "The pharmacist said when it comes to infants as young as Bowie, it's best not to overmedicate."

Put like that, Sierra could understand. But she could hardly bear to see the baby in such distress.

Shifting in the rocker, she started to lift Bowie to her shoulder, but Alex quickly bent and reached for him. "Here, let me have the little guy. I was the best belcher in the high school locker room. If anyone can get it out of him, I can."

Sierra didn't know whether to laugh or cry as she

handed the fussy baby over to Alex. "Just because you know how to rid yourself of gas doesn't mean you can make Bowie do it," Sierra argued. "He's a baby!"

Placing the infant against his broad shoulder, Alex began strolling around the large living room as he patted and rubbed Bowie's back in a circular motion.

Sierra watched Alex's tender ministrations and her heart clutched with something that felt soft and warm and terrifyingly like love.

No! That couldn't be, she silently denied. Wanting Alex in her arms was one thing, but loving him was something altogether different. He was a man who played fast and loose. In and out of the courtroom. She couldn't love a man who would never love her back.

As Alex completed another circle around the room, he paused by the rocker to toss Sierra a droll look. "Of course I know he's a baby," he said, attempting to raise his voice above the baby's wails. "And I'm not a dunce. I've seen all this stuff on television. You pat their back and soured milk spews out. Just give me time."

Alex had hardly spoken the last word, when a loud burp erupted from Bowie.

Putting a hand to her mouth, Sierra began to giggle. Alex twisted his head in an effort to see what sort of substance was running down the back of his shoulder.

"Oh, I'm so sorry about your shirt, Alex," Sierra said between laughs. "But you should have seen Bowie's face. He looked so surprised and relieved."

Alex grinned with inane pride. "Told you I could do it. Do you think that's all of it? The gas, I mean?"

Sierra left the rocker and headed toward the kitchen. "I don't know. Maybe you should pat him a little more and I'll get a towel for your shirt."

In the kitchen she grabbed paper towels and dampened a dish towel with warm water and soap. She was turning away from the sink when Alex appeared in the doorway. He mouthed the words "asleep" and with his free hand pointed to the baby.

Sierra walked quietly over to the two of them and peered at Bowie's face which was scrunched up against Alex's shoulder. The baby was snoozing peacefully as though he'd never experienced a moment of colic in his life.

Breathing a sigh of relief, Sierra nodded. "He's out like a light."

"What do I do with him now?"

Sierra wanted to laugh. For a man who'd seemed so confident about baby care a few minutes ago, he sure seemed lost now.

"Bring him into my bedroom and we'll put him to bed in the bassinet. Hopefully he'll stay asleep now that he's rid of some of that formula."

Putting down the things to clean his shirt, Sierra followed Alex to the bedroom and straightened the blankets in the little bassinet. Once she stepped out of the way, Alex carefully laid the sleeping baby onto the bed and covered him with a light blanket.

"He has dried milk around his mouth," Sierra whispered.

Alex turned wide, threatening eyes on her. "You're

not about to wake that little boy up just so that he can have a clean mouth," he said in a loud whisper. "He'll sleep just fine like that."

To make certain Sierra didn't try anything, Alex took her by the arm and led her out of the bedroom. Sierra left the door partly ajar so that they could hear the baby just in case he did wake up with another bout of colic.

"I'm so sorry about all of this, Alex. You've worked hard all day and you didn't plan on relaxing like this," she said.

Disappointment was evident in his green eyes as they roamed her face. "Why do you think you need to apologize for Bowie? We're in this together, aren't we?"

She hesitated, uncertain as to what he wanted to hear or what she needed to say. "Well...yes. I suppose we are. Without you I couldn't have kept Bowie. Child services believe you're going to be acting as his father."

His brows pulled together. "I *am* acting as his father, aren't I? I'm the closest thing to a daddy that the kid has right now."

Sierra's head tilted up and down in agreement, but her expression was clearly sad.

Seeing the woeful look on her face, Alex pulled her over to the couch and sat her down next to him. "What's the matter, you don't think I'm capable of being a daddy, is that it?"

She couldn't believe he was running off on a tangent like this. It wasn't like him. But then it wasn't like him to take her out to dinner or to care for a colicky baby, either.

This Alex was not the same sardonic friend who scolded her for having a mushy heart and useless boyfriends.

"No, Alex! That's hardly what I was thinking."

"Well, you had a damn miserable look on your face," he accused. "What was that all about?"

She shrugged one shoulder. The last thing she wanted to do was hurt his feelings. Especially after the closeness they'd shared in Red's courtyard.

"I was just thinking that you're only a part-time daddy for Bowie."

Something like regret tugged down the corners of his mouth and he looked away from her as he rubbed his hands against his thighs. "Yeah. Well, that's about par for the course, isn't it? An adopted kid wouldn't know how to be a real dad."

"Alex! Damn you!" she cried as she snatched a grip on his upper arm. "That's an awful thing to say. To imply something like that is to—you're insulting thousands of adopted men out there—"

"I'm not talking about other men," he interrupted sharply. "I'm talking about me." He plunked a finger into the middle of his chest. "I grew up living a lie. My own father didn't want me. And the man who raised me didn't have the guts to tell me the truth."

Her fingers tightened on his arm. "Oh, Alex, why are you bringing all this up now? I believed—" She paused as her brown eyes pleaded with him. "We were going to have a nice evening together. Bowie is asleep. And the house is quiet."

The soft, inviting tone of her voice got through to him

and the angry lines on his face slowly relaxed. Sierra sighed as he smiled and reached for her.

"God, I'm sorry, Sierra. I didn't mean to go off like that. We were coming home for other things, weren't we?" he asked with a throaty chuckle.

Her cheeks warmed with color as she nestled her head against his shoulder. "Bowie got us sidetracked."

Sierra slid her hands around to his back to slide closer, but suddenly her hand came in contact with something wet and gooey.

"Ugh! Your shirt!" Pulling away from him, she wrinkled her nose with disgust. "You've still got spit-up all over your back."

"Sorry," he said, then quickly suggested, "Maybe you should wipe it off for me."

Rising to her feet, Sierra held out a hand to him. "Maybe I should wash the whole shirt. Give it to me."

His jaw dropped as he feigned a look of shock, then with a wide, wicked smile, he stood and began to unbutton the blue, windowpane shirt. Starting with the bottom button and working his way to the top, his fingers maneuvered the fastenings until the fronts of the shirt fell away to expose a slice of male flesh.

Sierra's pulse rate nearly doubled and her mouth went desert dry as she watched him slip the garment from his shoulders and hand it to her.

As her fingers clutched the fabric, her eyes darted to the walls, the floor and the ceiling as she tried to avoid staring at his bare chest and arms, and the hard abs that disappeared beneath the waist of his chinos.

"What's the matter?" he asked, obviously amused at her reaction. "You look like you've never seen a man without a shirt on."

Heat filled her face and spread downward until it felt as if her whole body was blushing as she forced her eyes to meet with his. "Of course I have. But this…is…different. You're a friend."

Dimples bracketed his mouth as he stepped forward and slipped an arm around her waist. "And that just makes it all the nicer," he whispered.

Her heart was beating in her throat like a nervous little wren caught in the talons of a red-tailed hawk. And when he pulled the shirt from her hand and tossed it to the floor, she could hardly speak.

"Uh—would you like for me to find you another shirt?" she offered.

The amused look on his face turned into an all-out grin and he murmured in a voice as smooth as whiskey, "What I'd like won't require a shirt."

She groaned. Or had she whispered his name? Whatever had come out of her mouth didn't matter as Alex bent down and scooped her up in his arms.

"Bowie is in your bedroom. We don't want to wake him."

Sierra shook her head. "He sleeps soundly. We won't disturb him."

Assured by her answer, he began to carry her toward Sierra's bedroom.

Except for a faint strip of moonlight from the window, the room had grown very dark. Slipping through the shadows, Alex carefully made his way to the four-poster bed and placed Sierra onto the smooth yellow comforter.

For one wild second, as she watched his smiling face bending down to hers, she panicked. Oh, what was she doing? she desperately wondered. Alex was a playboy. This didn't mean anything to him. It was all fun and games.

Yet she couldn't roll away from him. She couldn't demand that he allow her up and out of the cozy bedroom. Like a deep craving that couldn't be denied, she had to kiss him, hold him and feel her naked body pressed against his.

"Sierra," he murmured as he moved up beside her and rubbed his nose alongside her heated cheek. "Why has it taken us so long to get here?"

Shifting toward him, she reached up and cradled the side of his face in her palm. "Are you even sure we should be here?" she asked softly.

He groaned and then brought his lips to hers. Sierra slipped her arm around his neck and snuggled closer against his chest. His skin was smooth, hot and filled her nostrils with a scent she'd come to recognize as simply Alex. It was a heady scent and she gathered it in her nostrils as her lips eagerly searched his.

"Doesn't it feel like we should be here?" Alex asked once he'd ended the kiss.

Sierra's breath was nearly gone and she waited a second for her head to stop spinning before she spoke. "It feels like magic, Alex. But—"

His nose and lips nuzzled the curve of her throat, the

back of her ear and finally her temple. "But what?" he asked. "Do you want this all to end? Are you afraid to make love with me?"

Make love with me. Yes, that was exactly what she would be doing, Sierra thought. She'd be making love with him straight from the center of her heart. She'd be giving him her body and soul. That was enough to make her terrified. And yet her fear, as strong as it was, still wasn't powerful enough to beat down the desire she felt for this man.

"No."

A sigh of relief rippled past his lips and brushed her cheek. "That's good. Because it would be hell to take my hands off you now."

Before she could make any sort of reply to that, Alex covered her mouth with another kiss. And after that, nothing else mattered. She didn't want to talk. She didn't want to worry or wonder how she'd feel once the sobering light of day arrived. Alex wanted her and she wanted him. That was enough for now.

As Alex kissed her, he could feel the struggle inside her collapse. Her body went limp, her mouth became even hungrier. The idea that she wanted him was a powerful aphrodisiac and his veins pulsed with heat and the throbbing need to be inside her.

Urgent now, his hands found the tie at her waist and tugged it loose. Her blouse had no buttons so as quickly as the sashes fell apart so did the front of the garment. She wasn't wearing a bra and Alex drew in a short, sharp breath as his eyes laid upon her small, perfectly made breasts.

"Oh, woman," he whispered, "how very beautiful you are."

Reverently his hand reached and cupped around the soft mound centered with a rosy-brown bud. Sierra moaned and arched toward him in silent need. Alex shifted so that his mouth was level with her breasts and for a moment he buried his face between them and breathed in the sweet, womanly scent of her skin, listened to the rapid beat of her heart as it shook her left breast and caused his own hands to tremble as they slid over her warm, satiny skin.

When his mouth finally touched her nipple, desire shot through him like an arc of electricity and he felt his loins tighten with overwhelming need, his manhood pulse. The strong, sudden reaction to the woman in his arms was shocking to Alex. Wanting a woman wasn't supposed to move this quickly!

Tearing his mouth from her breast, he reached to peel away the rest of her clothing, which consisted of only her skirt and a skimpy pair of pink panties. After tossing them to the floor, he dealt with his jeans and shoes. The items landed on top of Sierra's with a soft thud as he turned back to her.

"I hope you have some sort of birth control here," he said gently as he joined her on the queen-size mattress. "I don't go around prepared for such things."

Sierra reached for him and he growled with pleasure as she tugged him toward her. "I'm so very glad to hear that, Counselor. I thought you stayed prepared for this sort of thing."

"Hmm, you thought wrong," he said against her cheek.

"Well, don't worry. I'm covered."

His head reared back to look at her with stunned fascination. "I thought you said that you and Chad weren't lovers."

"We weren't. I have to—take oral contraceptives for other—monthly reasons," she explained.

A silly sort of relief rushed through him and he wondered why he was even thinking such thoughts. It didn't matter who Sierra had made love with in the past or how often. What mattered was this moment and each moment forward.

"Oh. I see. That's good. Real good."

"Is it?" she asked.

He slid his hands beneath her back and rolled her atop of him. With his palms cupping the flare of her hips, he said, "We already have one baby. We don't need another one right now."

We. We have a baby. His words sounded so sweet, so much like man-and-wife talk. Was he thinking of her in those terms? she wondered. No. She couldn't let herself imagine such a thing. She couldn't start letting herself believe that tonight was anything more than sex.

"Alex—" She paused as his hands slid upward and over the curved indention of her tiny waist, her ribs, and finally rested upon her shoulders. "I know that you've had lots of girlfriends and I—"

"Stop it. They have nothing to do with you and me. They're all in the past anyway. I don't have anyone in my life but you. Just you."

Her face dropped shyly away from his. "That's—that's not what's bothering me," she murmured.

He rested his head in the curve of her shoulder and speared his fingers into her hair. One by one, he pulled the pins until the long, curly mass spilled onto her shoulders and into his face.

"Oh, honey," he said gently. "There shouldn't be anything bothering you."

"I—I'm not very experienced, Alex. I've only done this once and that was a long time ago. And it—was just a rushed fumble in a college dorm room."

Rolling them both over, he placed her on her back and, propping his chin on the heel of his palm, studied her face in the semidarkness. All these years he'd known Sierra, he'd believed she'd been sharing "close" relationships with the boyfriends she'd paraded in front of him. To think that she'd gone so long without being intimate with anyone was shocking to him.

"Sierra, that's awful. Why? Why haven't you made love since? You've had boyfriends. Didn't they ever want—to be this close to you?"

Her face burned with embarrassment, but she didn't turn away or try to hide from him. She wanted him to know exactly how she was feeling. "Oh, yes, they wanted. I just wasn't ready to give. After that one time, I decided it would never happen again until I was with someone special, someone I trusted."

And that someone was him? Alex asked himself. The idea shook him down deep, in a spot that must have been dead before.

His heart swelled with tenderness as he reached to draw her closer. "Little darlin', I don't know what to say," he murmured as he brushed his fingertips against her temple. "Except that I'm glad you're not experienced. I'm glad that I'll be your first real lover."

Something between a sob and a laugh escaped her throat before she lifted her head from the mattress and latched her lips on to his.

After that, words weren't important. Hands searched and caressed while their kisses deepened and heated to a frantic mating of lips and tongues.

Sierra was caught up in a whirlwind that seemed to be going faster and faster as her body filled with heat, her mind shut down to everything except the wondrous magic of Alex's hands touching her breasts, her belly and thighs and the sweet mindless sensation of having their mouths connected.

Eventually his lips left hers and she sighed as his tongue began a measured, wet descent to the hollow of her throat, then farther on to the slope of one breast. As soon as his teeth closed gently around her excited nipple, she moaned and arched upward toward the mind-tingling pleasure.

"Alex—I—I didn't know it was supposed to feel this way!" she whimpered in astonishment.

Lifting his face, he saw her head writhing against the bed, her hair spread like tangled black vines around her face. Her eyes were closed, her sweet, wet lips twisted with something that was partly pleasure and partly pain.

Oh, but she was beautiful, he thought with renewed

wonder, a dark, erotic goddess who'd never been initiated into the art of making love. Just looking at her aroused him like nothing ever had. Every nerve, every muscle in his body was pulsing to the rhythm of his heartbeat. Sweat had misted his face and lathered his body. When he spoke his voice came out in a choked, guttural sound, "Neither did I, Sierra. Neither did I."

Dropping his head back to the opposite breast, he moistened the nipple with the tip of his tongue as his fingers worked a slow, wayward path to the soft curls nestled between her thighs.

Tensing with anticipation, Sierra clutched his muscled shoulders.

"Alex—"

"Shh. Don't be afraid, honey. I'm not going to hurt you. I'm going to love you. *Love you.*"

The last two words came out on a desperate groan. The erotic sound merged with Sierra's gasp as his fingers found the intimate folds of her womanhood and slipped inside.

Whimpering with need, she held on to him tightly until the ache in the lower part of her body became such a palpable throb she was certain every inch of her was going to burst into flames.

"I want you, Alex. Please, don't make me keep waiting," she pleaded.

With his face hovering over hers, he whispered against her lips. "Hold on to me, baby. Hold on and don't let go."

He entered her slowly and gently until their bodies

were completely united, but all too quickly the incredible sensation of being surrounded by her warmth and wetness overcame him and he began to move with deep, hungry thrusts.

For a moment, Sierra was stunned motionless by the unaccustomed invasion, but a few seconds was all it took before her body began to sing like a taut wire in a high wind.

Clasping her arms around his rib cage, she lifted her hips and met his mind-shattering thrust until both of their bodies were slick with sweat, their breathing fast and ragged. Yet she couldn't stop to get her breath or to even think. She had to find whatever it was that his body was offering. She had to put an end to the aching need that gripped her body.

When the climb finally ended, Sierra cried out softly as the room around them spun into a million tiny stars, shining and twirling all around them like jewels of passion.

The wonder of it stayed with her for long minutes, until finally the weight of Alex's body began to press her into the mattress and she squirmed for enough space to draw in a deep breath.

Sensing that he was squashing her, Alex rolled on the bed and pulled her along with him so that he could keep a hand on the curve of her waist.

With her eyes still closed, she rubbed her palms against his hair-roughened chest. "Mmm. You feel so good."

"You feel pretty incredible yourself," he replied with a tired smile.

Scooting closer, she pressed her cheek against the region of his heart. His hand ran down the back of her head and into her hair to make her lips tilt into a contented smile.

Bending his neck, Alex placed a kiss on her crown of black curls. "I'm sorry, honey. I didn't mean for that to happen so quickly. I wanted to give you more time."

Sierra had never felt so close, so drawn to any man as she did to Alex at this moment. "I didn't need more time."

He moved his head so that his cheek was resting against hers and she made a soft, mewing noise as his hands slid down her back and cupped her bottom. "Yes, you did. We both did. But you're just a bit too potent for me."

She giggled with disbelief, but Alex couldn't bring himself to laugh along with her. He was still too stunned, too dazed by what had just taken place between them. He'd expected making love with Sierra to be more than enjoyable. As far as physical pleasure went, he'd planned on it being very, very nice. He'd not expected it to be an earthquake. He'd not anticipated wanting her so quickly or so badly that he couldn't hold himself back.

She'd not just rattled Alex's body, she'd shaken his heart and that was the scariest part of it all.

"Alex?"

He felt her curvy little leg slide over his, her breasts press into his abdomen, and like a rewound clock he started to tick again.

"Yes."

"Uh—can we do it again?"

Chuckling under his breath, he took her face between his hands and brought his lips down to hers.

"Little wanton hussy."

Chapter Eight

The next morning Sierra awoke to sunlight streaming through the windows and the smell of fresh, strong coffee drifting into the bedroom.

Cracking one eye, she stretched, then suddenly remembering Bowie hadn't wakened her, she jerked her head toward the bassinet. It was gone!

Practically leaping out of bed, she wrapped a thin cotton robe around her naked body and raced out to the living room. One quick glance told her that part of the house was empty, so she trotted to the kitchen.

Halfway through the open door, she stopped dead in her tracks and stared at the sight before her. Alex had Bowie lying on a blanket spread upon the breakfast table and was in the process of changing the baby's diaper. Not just a wet diaper—a *dirty diaper.*

"Nice way to start a morning, huh?"

Obviously not hearing the approach of her bare feet, Alex looked up at the sound of her voice. A smile curved his lips as he took in her disheveled appearance.

"We're doing all right." He made a silly goo-goo face at Bowie. "Aren't we, baby boy?"

Tears were suddenly burning the back of Sierra's eyes and she didn't have a clue to why they were there. She only knew that something about the sight of Alex caring for Bowie was so sweet, so right that it touched the deepest part of her.

"Need any help?" She moved into the room and came to stand next to him.

He'd already rolled up the dirty disposable diaper and was fastening the new one around Bowie's tummy. Once it was secure, he picked up the offensive-smelling diaper as though it were a basketball and made a three-pointer in a trash can sitting several feet away.

"Nope. I think he's all set."

For good measure he reached for a container of baby powder and sprinkled it on the baby's legs. As Sierra watched his long, tanned fingers rub the talc into Bowie's skin, she couldn't help but recall how those same fingers had touched her last night, had turned her inside out with longing. Just thinking about their lovemaking heated her face. Especially now that they were facing each other in the light of day.

Stepping away from him, she hurried over to the cabinet. "I think I'll get some coffee. Have you had any yet?"

"Not yet. I've been too busy feeding Bowie."

Turning away from the cabinet, her brows lifted in surprise as she looked at him. "You've already fed Bowie?"

Alex gave her a smug smile. "Why, yes. You don't think I'd let the little fellow go hungry while his Sleeping Beauty mother lies in the bed, do you?"

Sierra glanced at the apple-shaped kitchen clock hanging over the double sink. It was only a quarter to seven. But his comment suddenly reminded her of how she must look to him this morning with her face bare, her hair tangled, her eyes puffy with sleep. Her appearance couldn't be a good sight. Whereas he looked as fresh as if he'd slept ten hours instead of a measly four.

Sierra pulled a sardonic face at him. "I'm hardly a Sleeping Beauty."

Chuckling at her early-morning testiness, Alex placed the baby in his infant carrier and propped him up to a sitting position. Once he was certain that Bowie was safe and satisfied, he walked over to where Sierra was stirring half-and-half into her coffee.

Pressing the front of his body to the back of hers, he slid his arms around her waist and linked his hands against her stomach. "You look like one to me," he murmured.

Sierra closed her eyes as she felt her bones melting, her heart filling with so much joy it terrified her.

"Hmm. I wonder who leads you around in the courtroom? I'm surprised you can find the judge's bench with that kind of eyesight."

"Ha, ha. You're so funny this morning. I didn't realize sleep turned you into a beautiful little monster."

Sierra found it impossible to keep a wide smile from her face as she turned in his arms and tilted her head back to look at him.

"What sleep?"

A chuckle rumbled deep in his chest. "I didn't hear you complaining."

Blushing, she pressed her cheek against his bare chest. The scent of his skin was an erotic reminder of the pleasure his body had given hers and the first stirrings of desire fluttered softly in the pit of her stomach. How could she be wanting him again, so soon? she wondered. Had he awakened some sort of dormant sex maniac?

"You've always accused me of being too easy. I guess last night proved just how easy."

He made a grunting sound of disapproval. "I hope you were teasing when you said that."

"I was," she replied, but silently she couldn't help wondering if she'd jumped into a deep pit without any hopes of ever climbing out. Alex was a bachelor. He'd never shown any sign that he was interested in marrying. He didn't want that close a relationship with any woman. So where did that leave her?

Stifling a sigh, she eased out of his embrace and turned to pick up her coffee. "Do you have court today?" she asked as she carefully sipped the hot drink.

Alex watched her swipe a fumbling hand at the black

hair falling into her face. She looked so sweet and vulnerable and he realized that her softness, her easygoing heart, the very things he'd chided her about were exactly the things that were drawing him to her now. From his perspective, none of that made sense. But he felt it all the same.

"Ten, this morning. One, this afternoon. I'll be at the courthouse most of the day." He glanced at the clock. "And by the way, I'd better be going. I've got some depositions to go over before trial this morning. And Pauline will give me hell if I'm late."

"Wouldn't you like some breakfast? I'll cook you some hotcakes with pecan syrup and peppered bacon."

Because cooking was second nature to Sierra, Alex knew that she considered the offer a simple thing. Yet it touched him in an odd, silly way that made his chest swell and his heart smile.

Closing the small distance between them, he planted a kiss on her forehead. "Thank you, darlin', but I don't have time."

She sighed. "Okay."

He lifted a black curl from her shoulder and brought it to his lips. "Don't look so disappointed. I'll be back this evening."

Her brows shot up. "This evening?"

Amusement dimpled his cheeks. "Yes, tonight. After work. Why? You'd rather not have me around?"

Her brown eyes darkened with concern as her hand fluttered in a helpless gesture against his chest. "Of course I—you know that I want you around. But, Alex, what is—what does this mean?"

The pads of his fingers slid gently underneath her jaw as he studied her troubled face. "It means that I want to be with you." Bending his head, he pressed several kisses to her cheek, her nose and her forehead. "In fact, I think I might bring a razor and a pair of khakis with me. I might need them if I stay overnight."

A stunned look came over her face, but Alex figured she couldn't be nearly as surprised at the suggestion as he was of it himself. He'd never set out to charm Sierra, to seduce her and turn their relationship into something far more than friends. The whole thing had happened as though fate had taken hold of his hand and he couldn't break away.

"Sierra, you're not saying anything. What do you think? Can I hang my trousers in your closet?"

She was probably heading straight to Heartbreak Pass. It wasn't written anywhere on this earth that Alex would stay around a day longer than any of her past boyfriends. But then Alex was more than a boyfriend. As of last night, he'd become her lover. She adored him and probably had for years now. There was no way that she could ever deny herself the pleasure of having him close.

"I'll make room."

An hour later, Sierra, showered and dressed in a fluttery gauze dress and high-heel sandals, called the Stocking Stitch to ask her mother if she could watch Bowie for a few hours while Sierra filled in at the social services office for another co-worker.

"Oh, Sierra, I would in a minute," Maria said with disappointment. "But I've got two knitting classes today and both of them are filled to the brim. Why don't you drive out to Rosita's? She'd love to watch Bowie for you."

Normally, since Sierra was on leave, the office wouldn't have called her. But several employees were out for different reasons and the staff was operating very shorthanded. Sierra didn't mind working for a few hours. As long as she knew Bowie was being well cared for.

"She's not going to be attending classes with you today?"

"No. And she's not down at the big Fortune house today, either. I talked to her earlier this morning. She's home, getting some sort of special dinner ready for Cruz. I'll call her and warn her that you're coming," Maria insisted.

Sierra sighed. She didn't really have the time to drive all the way out to the Double Crown Ranch, but there wasn't really anyone else around who she would trust to care for Bowie.

"All right, Mom. I'm heading out there now. And thanks."

"Before you go, Sierra, how did your dinner date go last night? You and Alex left the restaurant so early!"

It was a good thing Sierra wasn't hooked up to one of those video cameras that allowed the caller a view of the person they were having a conversation with. Otherwise her mother would see that her daughter's face was beet red.

"Uh, well, it wasn't all that early. We wanted to get home to watch a certain program on television. Then Bowie had a bout of colic. But we had a nice evening. I've got to go now, Mom, or I'm going to be late."

"Bowie had colic? Oh dear, how did Alex handle all that crying?"

Like a real father, Sierra thought. For a man who'd never had siblings or been around babies, he seemed to have a natural instinct for dealing with Bowie. He handled the baby with loving ease, as though he was meant to be a daddy, not just to Bowie, but to several children. Yet she sensed that he would laugh at the very idea.

"He handled it better than I did. Bye, Mom."

She hung up before her mother could question her further. She didn't want to slip up and give her mother any idea that Alex had spent the night with her. Not that she would be angry about it, Sierra thought. In fact, she figured her mother would be pleased to hear that her daughter and Alex had gotten "close." But Maria would put far too much importance on the whole affair.

Affair. Sierra had always hated the word and she didn't like it any better this morning. She didn't want to label her relationship with Alex as something purely sexual and short-lived. But what else could it be? she wondered glumly.

A few minutes later, Sierra was driving south, toward the Double Crown Ranch. With Red Rock behind her, the landscape opened up to short, rolling hills and green pastures dotted with spreading live oak and pecan trees.

When Sierra reached a side entrance to the ranch, she pulled through a cattle guard flanked by tall clusters of blooming pampas grass and purple sage. Off to the left, surrounded by a sandstone wall, the Double Crown ranch house sat like a Western-style castle beneath towering cottonwoods and spreading live oaks.

The sight never failed to stir Sierra and she rested her foot on the brake as she paused to take a gander at the home of one of the most famous families in south Texas.

The adobe structure had a flat roof supported by heavy wooden beams and covered with terra-cotta-colored tiles. Wrought-iron gates opened onto a fabulous courtyard where the grounds were kept immaculate and always blooming with bougainvillea, roses and hibiscus. Sierra considered the inside of the house to be even more majestic than the grounds outside and she'd never forget as a child how intimidated she'd felt when she'd attended her first social function in the grand home.

Now that she'd grown up, she realized the Fortunes weren't snobs. In fact, most of them were always helping some person or some worthy cause. Sadly, down through the years, there had been much tragedy in the family. Sierra could only hope the Fortune heartbreak didn't spill onto her sister once Gloria married Jack.

Sierra lifted her foot from the brake and pressed on the gas. As the car moved forward, she said to the baby, who was strapped into the back seat and happily nursing on a pacifier, "Just think, Bowie, my sister is marrying into the Fortune family. They're rich and famous. That's nice. But it's not my style. I'd rather just have you and me and Alex in the old two-story."

Realizing how matrimonial that sounded, she shook the dreamy image from her mind. Alex might want to share her bed and her closet from time to time. But he wouldn't be there forever. She was smart enough to prepare herself for reality.

Rosita and Ruben's small ranch house was situated a short distance down the road from the ranch yard where cattle and horses were penned and cared for. The Perezes had worked for Ryan Fortune for many years and Rosita especially was very close to the whole family. It was obvious this would be the couple's home for the rest of their lives.

Sierra passed several barns and corrals before she eventually turned onto a short graveled driveway that led to the Perez home. Before she could unbuckle Bowie from his safety seat, Rosita was out the front door and ambling out to the car to greet her.

If Rosita lived to be a hundred, Sierra doubted her appearance would change. For as long as she could remember, Rosita had worn her black hair pulled straight back into a bun. Even the gray streak at the temple had remained the same size and color over the years. Her thick middle was a result of her delicious cooking, just as the warm smile on her face was a product of her huge heart.

"Sierra, I was so happy when Maria called a few minutes ago. I've been wanting to see this baby of yours. Where is he?"

The older woman grabbed Sierra and gave her a tight hug. Sierra hugged her back and kissed the housekeeper's smooth brown cheek. "He's in the back. I'll get him out."

After Sierra unbuckled the baby from the car seat, she placed him over in the smaller carrier before she finally lifted him out of the car.

With a pleased smile on her face, Sierra presented the baby to Rosita. The older woman quickly inspected him, then waved an admonishing hand at her.

"No. No, Sierra. You shouldn't be carrying the baby like this. Let me have the precious one and I'll show you how to hold him like a baby should be held."

Before Sierra could react, Rosita dug the baby out of the plastic carrier and cradled him against her soft, ample bosom. "Now see," she said to Sierra. "He feels strong arms around him, a warm breast next to his cheek. Those are the things a baby longs for when he comes into the world. That will never change—no matter how many plastic contraptions there are in the stores."

"Yes, I'm sure you're right, Rosita," Sierra agreed. "But the carrier supports his back and neck."

Rosita rolled her brown eyes as if to say the younger generation was so misguided. "A piece of cold plastic is not what he needs. How would you like to be laid out on a board? You use your arms and your hands to support him. He needs to learn the smell and the feel of his mother. It will make him feel safe and loved."

Since Rosita had raised several children of her own and was now helping care for her grandchildren, Sierra couldn't doubt her experience in caring for babies.

"Okay, Rosita, I won't use the carrier unless I'm going to set him somewhere."

Grinning with approval, Rosita looked down at the baby. "He's a handsome guy, Sierra," she said, then immediately shook her head in disbelief. "What sort of woman could turn away from something so precious?"

"Not a woman, Rosita. A young teenager, who wasn't even capable of caring for herself."

Rosita smoothed a finger across the baby's cheek. "Well, at least she had sense enough to give the child to you." Turning toward the house, she motioned for Sierra to follow. "Bring his things."

Once inside the small, neat house, Rosita sat down on the couch. Sierra needed to be back on the road, but she'd not spoken to Rosita in a while, and she didn't want to be rude. Not when the woman was so generously helping her out with Bowie.

Easing down onto the seat of an easy chair, she said, "You're so sweet to watch him for me like this, Rosita. Mom said you were going to be busy cooking today. I hope this isn't going to interrupt your work."

Rosita laughed. "You think I don't know how to take care of a baby and cook at the same time?"

Sierra laughed along with the other woman. "I guess that was silly of me, wasn't it."

The Fortunes longtime housekeeper passed a keen gaze over Sierra's appearance. "We haven't talked in a long time. Not since your two sisters came home. Are you glad they're back?"

"Rosita!" Sierra exclaimed with a shocked laugh. "How could you ask me such a question? Gloria and Christina are my sisters. Of course I'm glad they're back home. And you *know* how my parents feel about having them near again. I don't think I've ever seen them so happy. Especially with Gloria planning her wedding and Christina getting engaged."

The older woman's lips pursed with disapproval as she continued to study Sierra. "Gloria and Christina aren't the only ones in the family. Maria and Jose have another daughter, too, you know. Their world doesn't just revolve around two of their five children."

Dropping her head, Sierra stared blankly at her linked fingers. "I understand that, Rosita. I just meant that— well, Gloria and Christina have had all sorts of problems and heartaches whereas I've just been little ol' me. Nothing my parents need to worry about."

The tsking of Rosita's tongue told Sierra that the other woman was a little disgusted with her, although she didn't understand why. Sierra was the one who'd come straight home from college to be with her parents, to help them with the restaurant, illnesses, family matters, anything that they needed help with. Sierra was the one who'd worn herself to a frazzle trying to patch the rift between her sisters and keep peace in the family. Most of the time during that period her private life had suffered greatly.

"But they do worry about you, Sierra. They want

you to be happy, too. You have proved your love and dedication to them over and over. Don't think they ever forget that."

Regret saddened Sierra's features as she looked at the other woman. "Sometimes I feel awful, Rosita. Sometimes I resent how my sisters ran off from home and responsibilities and left everything to me. And now—it looks like they've been rewarded for their past bad behavior. Gloria is pregnant and marrying into the Fortune family. Christina will marry a Rockwell. And me— well, why does life happen this way, Rosita? Is it fair?"

The older woman smiled gently at Sierra. "You know the old saying, Sierra. The only fair is one with cows and pigs. But you're not to worry. I had a dream about you the other night."

Like Sierra had told Alex at dinner the other night, Rosita had been having dreams and intuitions for years. The ones that came true always left an eerie chill down Sierra's back. She honestly didn't want to know what Rosita had dreamed about her for fear that it really would come to pass. "Really?"

Glancing down at Bowie, Rosita shifted the baby to a more comfortable position in her arms and then she looked up to pin her dark, serious gaze on Sierra.

"Yes. I dreamed that you would become a wife before your two sisters married."

Sierra sucked in a shocked breath and then, the longer she thought about it, a laugh erupted from deep in her throat.

"Rosita! Have you been getting into Ryan Fortune's

wine collection? I believe you're nipping the sauce. Or you must have had indigestion the night you had that dream. I'm not even engaged."

"You have a fella, don't you?" Rosita countered, clearly irritated that Sierra was fluffing off her important dream.

Sierra started to say no, Chad had left her in the dust. But Chad had never been her fella in the real sense of the word. Making love with Alex had shown her just how shallow her feelings had been toward the man.

"Uh, yes. Sort of." After last night Alex felt like her man. At least she had to believe he'd be her man for a while. Knowing Alex's fleeting relationships, that was the best she could hope for.

"Then you mark my word. You'll be kneeling before the priest, saying your vows very soon."

Unsettled by Rosita's strange prediction, Sierra quickly rose to her feet and grabbed the diaper bag holding all the baby's necessities. "I'm—I'm running late for work, Rosita. Let me show you about mixing Bowie's formula and then I've got to be going."

More than an hour later, Sierra was sitting at her desk, going over a family visitation report, when a co-worker paused beside her chair.

She looked up to see Vivian, a divorced, middle-aged redhead, who Sierra could always count on as a friend. The woman had worked for social services for many years and had been a veteran when Sierra had started out as a green field officer. The stressful toll showed in

Vivian's faded blue eyes and the cynical droop of her mouth, and oftentimes when Sierra looked at her friend, she wondered if that's what trying to help people did to a person. Drained the very life from them. While her sisters had been gone from the family it had certainly taken a toll on Sierra's outlook.

"Hi, Viv. What's up?"

The other woman's smile was a bit hesitant. "I'm glad you came in today. I tried to call you yesterday, but you must have been out of the house."

Sierra turned the swivel chair so that she was facing Vivian. The woman placed a short envelope on the corner of the desk.

"What's that?"

"A letter from Ginger's mother. At least that's what the return says. I didn't open it. It came here to the department, but it's addressed to you."

An uneasy feeling hit Sierra's stomach as she reached for the envelope and slowly slipped the top open with a fingernail file.

"Do you think she wants Bowie back?" Vivian asked, as she worriedly chewed on her bottom lip. "Or maybe Ginger wants him back and she's too afraid to approach you about him."

Just the idea of having her baby taken away made Sierra quake with fear. He was beginning to feel more and more like a child that she'd actually given birth to. Especially now that Alex was sharing the baby with her.

"I don't know—just let me read," Sierra answered in a strained voice.

The letter was short and to the point, the grammar and spelling not even close to being correct. But the words were full of emotion and after a moment Sierra was forced to close her eyes and blink back tears.

Placing a supportive hand on Sierra's shoulder, Vivian asked in a hurried rush, "What's the matter?"

Shaking her head, Sierra dabbed at her eyes and sniffed. "It's just so sad, Viv. To think of any woman living like Mrs. Rollins is forced to live."

"What do you mean, Sierra? The woman isn't forced," Vivian said mockingly. "She chose the loser husband who enjoys slapping her around. She could definitely get rid of him if she wanted to."

Sierra glared at her co-worker's pessimistic attitude. "Viv! Since when did you become so heartless? The woman is trying to get rid of him without getting herself killed. And that's what she says in this letter. She and Ginger don't want the baby to be in the Rollinses' home. She says they love him too much to see his life ruined and they know he'll get a good life with me."

The last part of Mrs. Rollins's message had left Sierra feeling very humble and weepy. She didn't understand why the two women had considered her to be the right person to raise Bowie, but they had, and she couldn't help feeling proud and immensely relieved.

Vivian suddenly looked deflated. "Oh. Well, I'm glad about the baby." She cast a guilty glance at Sierra. "And that part about Mrs. Rollins doing better, I know that she's trying. And I realize it's hard for her. I guess—I'm just getting hard-nosed." She sighed with weary regret.

"When you see so much abuse and poverty over and over for years, you tend to get hard, Sierra. You'll learn that after you've been here several more years."

Sierra didn't think so. If she ever stopped really caring for the people she was trying to help, then she would know it was time to get out of the job.

Patting Vivian's hand, she said, "Maybe you should take a little time off, Viv. You could go on a nice long vacation. Heaven knows you've paid your dues here. I can't remember the last time you took even a day away from work."

Vivian batted a hand through the air and smiled. "Oh, don't worry about me, Sierra. I haven't burned out yet. What I'd like to know, though, is what you're going to do about Bowie?"

Ignoring the ringing telephones and the workers bustling through the aisles of cubicles that served as offices, Sierra put the letter away and looked at her friend. "What sort of question is that?"

"A normal one, I'd think. You're a young, beautiful woman and you're single. Do you really think you want to be saddled with a child? And when you meet the right man, he might not want to raise someone else's child, he might only want his own flesh and blood. Then what sort of problems are you going to have on your hands?"

Her lips pressed together, Sierra turned the chair back to her desk and picked up the file she'd been reading. "Viv, I wouldn't allow a man like that to live in my doghouse, much less close to me."

"Oh, come on, Sierra. You know what I'm trying to say."

Sierra sighed. She loved Vivian, but sometimes the woman was like sandpaper scratching a blackboard.

"I know that any man who wouldn't accept a child of mine would be crossed off my list," Sierra said flatly.

"Well, I suppose a woman who looks like you can afford to be choosey when it comes to men. The rest of us have to kowtow."

Groaning, Sierra said, "Not hardly. Besides, I—well, I already have someone in my life. And he loves Bowie."

Vivian's eyes popped wide, but before she could fire any questions at Sierra, the office manager stuck her head around Sierra's cubicle and ordered the other woman to her office.

Once Vivian was gone, Sierra tried her best to get back into the file she'd been going over, but some of what Vivian had been saying kept popping up in her thoughts. Sierra realized that there were men in the world who refused to raise another man's child. But she couldn't imagine Alex having such a selfish attitude. After all, he was adopted himself. He knew how important it was for a baby to be given a good home and family. And he seemed so attached to Bowie. If she did decide to adopt Bowie, would Alex stand beside her? she wondered. Oh God, she hoped so. Because she was beginning to realize that she couldn't give up either one of them.

Chapter Nine

A week later, Alex was sitting in his office contemplating a lunch of tuna sandwich and a bag of potato chips when Pauline sounded off from the room next door.

"Alex, your mother is on the line."

Since the office was empty, Pauline preferred to use the strength of her lungs rather than the intercoms on their desks. Like a blow horn, her voice nearly rattled the windows.

"I've got it," he called back to his secretary and with a heavy sigh he punched in line two and picked up the receiver.

He wasn't in the mood to talk to his mother. He'd had a particularly rough morning in court defending a man who'd been accused of stealing from his business partner. And once the lunch recess was over, he was facing an even rougher afternoon with a hostile witness. For the first time he could ever remember, he honestly wasn't looking forward to the courtroom sparring between lawyers and judge. He'd rather be home with Sierra and the baby.

"Hello, Mom."

"Hi, honey. I hope I'm not interrupting. Pauline said you had a minute or two."

Alex couldn't deny his mother was a lovely woman. At fifty, Emily Calloway's face was nearly line free, her reddish-brown hair threaded with only a handful of gray and her figure trim and fit. On the inside, she was equally pretty, and since Alex had grown up and moved away, she'd spent most of her time trying to help the less fortunate people of Dallas.

His father, Dave Calloway, was a successful businessman and had made a fortune in the construction business in and around the Forth Worth-Dallas area. He was a gentle, good-hearted man who'd worked hard to see that his wife had anything she needed, along with his son.

His son. But he wasn't actually Dave Calloway's son. Alex's real father was out there someplace, a man whom he would never see, but someone whose genes and blood ran through his body.

"Alex? Are you there? Hello?"

Shaking his head, Alex pinched the bridge of his nose and tried to concentrate on his mother's voice. "Yeah. Sorry, Mom. I—I've got a lot on my mind."

"Your work?"

Not exactly, he thought. His work was always un-predictable and stressful. He was accustomed to the chaotic schedule. Frankly, he was worried about himself, about Sierra and, last but not least, little Bowie. Spending more time with her and the baby had seemed like the logical thing to do. He wanted to be with them. But he'd not expected staying under the same roof with a woman and a baby would have such an impact on him. He'd not expected to feel so happy, so peaceful and settled. That wasn't like him at all, and it scared the hell out of him to think that it was all going to end.

But Alex didn't want to share any of those thoughts with his mother. It was all too fresh, too personal to pour out to anyone.

"Uh—yeah," he answered. "Tough trial. But it's nothing to worry about."

"Well, I won't keep you long, Alex. I was just wondering when you might be driving up to Dallas? We haven't seen you in a long time and your dad's birthday is at the end of the month. We'd love to have you with us for the celebration."

Closing his eyes for a brief moment, Alex swallowed at the wad of emotions trying to collect in his throat. Damn it, the two people he'd loved so much, whom he'd trusted with all his heart and soul, had lied to him. Over the years, he'd tried to forget and forgive them for the deceit. And he had forgiven them. His parents loved him; he couldn't doubt that. But the two of them had never realized what their deception had done to him or how it constantly guided his decisions.

"I'd love to be with you, too. But I don't think I'll be able to make a hole in my schedule. I'll have Pauline to see what's lined up for that date, though," he added, to soften her disappointment.

"Oh."

He could hear her sigh and it made him feel awful. Hell, being around Sierra was making him soft; as soft as a pat of warm butter.

"Well, it's good that your business has picked up that much. Maybe Dad and I could drive down to San Antonio. That way you wouldn't have to do anything except put up with us for a night or two."

Oh Lord. He might as well spit out the truth. "Uh— Mom. I don't—I'm not always living at my apartment."

"*Whaaat?* What's happened?"

Five foot three inches of sugar and spice, Alex thought. Aloud, he said, "Nothing. I still have the apartment. I'm just—spending a lot of time with someone else now."

"A woman."

He could hear the excitement rattling her voice.

"Naturally."

Emily chuckled. "Naturally? You've never mentioned staying overnight with a woman before. What does this mean?"

Of course she'd have to ask, he thought wryly. And how did she expect him to answer when he had no idea what it meant? Except that he was crazy about Sierra. And Bowie, too.

"Don't start jumping the gun, Mom. We're taking things slowly." Yeah, right. He'd gone from being her friend to her lover all in the matter of one night. That was a real snail's pace.

"Well, this is wonderful news, son. Maybe I can finally look forward to some grandchildren," she said with another suggestive chuckle.

Alex wasn't about to give his mother a hint about Bowie. She'd be on a plane tomorrow to see him. "Mom, I really have to go. I've got to be back in court in twenty minutes and I haven't finished my lunch yet." He paused, pinched the bridge of his nose, then added, "And as for Dad's birthday, I'll try to make it up there somehow."

"Wonderful, son! I love you. Bye now."

"I love you, too, Mom."

Alex tossed the receiver onto the hook and let out a weary sigh. What in hell was happening to him? It wasn't like him to cave in to someone else's wants and wishes. He normally put his own needs first. After all, who was going to take care of him if he didn't? But the whole time his mother had been speaking, he'd been thinking how disappointed Sierra would be with him if he didn't make an effort to observe his father's birthday.

Raking both hands through his brown hair, he stared blankly at the view of the street beyond the windows. Did he love Sierra? he wondered. Did he want to marry her? The questions sent something like panic rushing through him, but like a witness facing a judge, he had to at least try to answer honestly.

And the truth was, he couldn't imagine not having Sierra in his life. He'd known her since he was nineteen years old and through the years he'd never let their relationship drift apart. Even though she drove him batty with frustration at times, he'd always wanted her company. Maybe something had always been trying to tell him that she was supposed to be *his* woman.

But Alex had never been good with the idea of loving a woman. Hell, he even had trouble keeping a real, true friend around for more than a year or two. Oh, there were Trey, Mario and Gayle, but they were just people to laugh and have a beer with once a week. Sierra was the only one of the bunch he'd ever hung out with outside their lunch meeting.

Sierra. Sierra. Always Sierra.

"Alex! Have you seen a UFO? You're in a trance!"

The sound of Pauline's harsh scolding jerked Alex out of his thoughts and caused him to outwardly flinch as though a bomb had gone off in the outer office.

"Pauline, damn it, I've got trial in—" he paused long enough to glance down at his wrist "—ten minutes!"

Jumping up from the desk chair, he grabbed his notes, stuffed them into a black leather briefcase and adjusted his tie. "I've gotta get going."

Leaving the desk, he jogged toward the door with Pauline racing right on his heels. "Alex, I'm making you a doctor's appointment!" she exclaimed. "You're sick. You're not yourself!"

With Pauline yelling after him, Alex hurried around the building to his SUV. As he started the vehicle and headed down the street to the courthouse, he wondered if his secretary was right. Maybe he was sick. Lovesick. Maybe that's the reason he couldn't get Sierra out of his mind for more than five minutes at a time. Or why every night he couldn't wait to get home to make love with her.

No. God help him, no. He couldn't be in love. He didn't want to feel *that* close to a woman. If he did, he'd have to start trusting her. He'd have to believe that she would always be honest with him and he wasn't at all sure that he could ever do that again.

Sierra hummed along to a song on the radio as she set plates onto the table and stirred jambalaya on the gas range. Outside the kitchen, rain poured from the roof of the porch and splashed onto her boxes of tomato plants.

Darkness had fallen a few short minutes ago and she knew Alex would be arriving home soon. The knowledge filled her heart with joy and she realized that each day she spent with him was more precious than the last.

"Mmm. Mmm. Something smells good."

As Alex entered the warm kitchen, he spotted Sierra stirring a pot on the range. A pair of worn blue jeans fit snugly against her pert little bottom and shapely legs. A halter made of red bandana material was tied against her smooth brown back and the sexy sight of her was enough to push away his mental fatigue.

With the sound of the rain masking his footsteps, Alex came up behind her and slipped his hands around her bare waist.

Squealing, she whirled around and the second she realized it was him, the shock on her face turned to a happy smile.

Rising on her tiptoes, she reached to hug him. "Hello, Counselor," she said.

Having Sierra back in his arms was like a long cool drink after a broiling hot day. He bent his head and murmured against her ear. "Hello, yourself. Did you miss me?"

"Terribly," she teased. "I cried all day."

He gave her bottom a playful little pinch, then before she realized his intentions, he stooped down and scooped her up in his arms.

Her gasp of surprise was smothered beneath the hungry kiss he planted on her lips.

"Where's Bowie?" he finally whispered.

She pointed toward the living room. "In his bassinet. Asleep. Why?"

The half grin on his face was wicked and tempting, the glint in his eyes making all sorts of delicious promises and Sierra's heart began to chug with heavy, rapid beats.

"Because I can't wait to make love with you. Turn off the stove. We'll eat later," he ordered huskily.

Since they were already standing close to the range, Sierra reached down and switched off the burner beneath the jambalaya. As soon as that was done, Alex carried her to the bedroom and left the door open so they could hear Bowie, just in case he cried.

Shadows darkened the bed and the rain had left the room cooler than normal. Alex placed Sierra in the middle of the mattress, then starting with his loosened tie began to shed his clothing.

Sierra watched him for a few moments until he reached to pull down his trousers and by then she was aching for him so badly she hurried to remove her own clothing.

"Oh, darling," she whispered as he lowered himself down next to her. "Hurry! I can't wait."

Spurred by her pleas, he covered her lips with his and plunged his manhood deep within her. The sudden sensation of being inside her tight, moist folds rocked him like an explosion and his head fell back as a rough groan rumbled up from his chest.

Somewhere in his heated daze, he felt her legs wind around his, her hands clasp his hips. He began to thrust fiercely as the need to possess her, to become a part of her, overrode everything.

Sierra matched the rhythm of his body and soon their skin became slick with sweat, their breathing raspy and uneven. His lips clung to hers as he pushed his tongue past her teeth and tasted the sweet, intimate cavity of her mouth.

Sliding one hand beneath her back, he lifted her slightly from the mattress so that her breasts would touch his chest, her tight nipples would tease his skin. She moaned and slid her hands upward so that she could hold on and keep the contact of their upper bodies.

Outside, rain continued to drum on the roof and, like the rain, Alex wished he could go on and on, making love with Sierra until his mind was blank, his heart content.

But the richness of her body was almost too much for him to bear and before long he felt the pressure in his loins building, building until he couldn't hold back his release. With a guttural cry, he grabbed her buttocks and lifted her even closer.

Like a vortex of whipping winds, he felt the room around them begin to whirl, the breath being sucked from his lungs. He heard her desperate cries and knew that he could wait no longer.

Burying his face in the side of her neck, he felt the very essence of him pour into her body.

Afterward he rolled away and tried to quickly fill his empty lungs. Inches away, Sierra waited until her own breathing had calmed before she turned on her side to face him.

"Are you all right?" she asked quietly.

He didn't answer immediately and she passed a hand over his damp chest. The soft hair curled around her fingers and she pulled it gently as she waited for his response.

"Sure. Why do you ask?"

A worried groove appeared between her brows. "I don't know. You just seem—a little desperate tonight."

Funny that she should use that word, Alex thought. Because that was exactly how he was feeling: fraught, anxious and desperate to have her.

"I'm okay, Sierra. Don't worry about me."

Rolling closer, she snuggled her cheek upon his chest. "You're not feeling ill, are you?"

He stroked her back and savored the velvet smoothness of her skin. "No. But Pauline thinks I'm sick. I didn't tell her that making love with you every night is wearing me down."

She studied him for long moments as she waited for

him to say more. When he didn't, she decided to tell him about the letter she'd received from Mrs. Rollins.

"That's good," Alex said once she was finished. "At least now you know the Rollinses won't be yelling for custody anytime soon."

Hopefully they would never yell to get custody of Bowie, Sierra thought. But she didn't say more on the subject. Right now she was more concerned with Alex's melancholy mood.

She trailed her fingers along his damp abs and up along his rib cage. "Hmm, tomorrow night when you come in, I'm sending you straight to the recliner and I'll carry your supper to you."

A soft chuckle shook his chest. "Sounds like you're going to try to spoil me."

"You're worth it," she said gently. Then, lifting her head, she began to press slow, moist kisses over his shoulder and up the side of his neck.

With a groan, he reached for her and wrapped her body next to his. "Baby, baby. The things you do to me."

Her lips reached his jaw and she paused long enough to slide her tongue against the faint stubble of his beard. "Well, we could get up and eat jambalaya."

Turning his face into hers, he whispered against her lips, "The jambalaya can wait."

The next morning, Sierra drove to San Antonio to shop at Babies Unlimited, a boutique on the river walk that sold everything from clothing and diaper pins, to baby beds and infant swings.

For the past week, she'd been slowly attempting to transform the bedroom next to hers into a nursery. She'd papered the walls with a clown print, dressed the windows with blue-and-white checked curtains and used the same material to skirt the bassinet. All she lacked now to make it usable was a baby bed and she wanted the crib to be a special one.

After the rainstorm that had swept through the night before, the morning had turned clear and gorgeous. Hot sunshine beat down on her arms and neck as she slowly pushed Bowie along the water's edge in his new stroller.

"Sierra! Sierra, is that you?"

Hearing the female voice some distance behind her, Sierra stopped to look and was surprised to see her sister Gloria waving at her.

"What are you doing here?" she asked as she sauntered gracefully up to Sierra.

As usual, Gloria was dressed adorably in a snappy green spring suit and her makeup was as perfect as her hair. Compared to her older sister, Sierra felt dowdy in her casual jeans and ponytail. But Alex thought she was beautiful. At least he told her she was and that was all that Sierra needed.

"I'm going to Babies Unlimited. What are you doing?" She glanced at her wristwatch. "Why aren't you at work?"

Gloria's nose crinkled playfully. "I am at work. But I had an assistant take over for a few minutes. I wanted to see what sort of nursery furniture Babies Unlimited had to offer. Can you believe the two of us had the same idea this morning?"

Her sister rounded the stroller and squatted down to Bowie's level. "Aw, Sierra, he's getting more precious every day." She picked up his tiny hand and kissed it. "He's really going to be a handsome guy."

Sierra's heart swelled with love and pride. "I think so."

Rising back to her full height, Gloria motioned toward an empty park bench that was shaded by the drooping limbs of a nearby willow. "Let's sit down a minute," she suggested. "Before we walk on to the boutique."

Sierra followed her sister and once they were settled on the bench, Gloria reached for her hand and squeezed it. "I've been thinking about you a lot lately, sis. How are things going? Has having Bowie around helped you to get Chad out of your system?"

Sierra very nearly laughed. If only Gloria could see how her life had changed since Alex had been spending some of his nights with her. For the first time, she felt like a woman, she felt important to someone.

"Chad Newbern is just a wisp of a memory. I'm doing—great. Really great," she added with a smile.

"That must be true," Gloria said as she inspected Sierra's glowing face. "You must be sleeping better these days."

Once again, Sierra felt a laugh bubble up in her throat. What would her sister think if she told her about the wickedly delicious nights she'd been spending in Alex's arms? Sleep had been the last thing on her mind.

"Oh, much better. I can't understand it, but it's been days since I've had to get up and drink a cup of warm milk or read a book," she said as normally as she could.

"That's good to hear. It must be the baby," she reasoned. "I don't have to ask. I can see how much you love Bowie. And that's what I've been thinking about—wondering what you plan to do about him."

Sierra frowned. "Right now, he's my foster child."

Gloria nodded with concern. "Yes. But is that enough for you? What if social services wants to place him elsewhere?"

"They could. But I don't see any reason for them to do that."

"You're a single mother," Gloria reasoned. "They might find a regular family to take him."

She and Alex were a regular family, Sierra thought. At least as regular as a man and woman could be without being married. But she wasn't yet ready to confess to her sister that Alex had been staying part of the time with her or that she could fall in love with the independent lawyer.

Glancing down at the sluggish flow of the narrow river, Sierra said with a thread of defiance, "I can give Bowie everything he needs."

"Okay. So what if his mother decides she wants him back? You would be crushed."

That scenario had gone over and over in Sierra's mind and each time she thought about Ginger trying to reclaim Bowie, she shook with fear.

But she had Ginger's note and Mrs. Rollins's letter, she tried to assure herself. Both of which voiced their wishes to have Sierra be Bowie's mother. That would surely carry some major weight with child care services or in a court of law.

Her expression troubled, Sierra looked at her sister. "What are you trying to say, Gloria? You think I should give Bowie up?"

Gloria quickly shook her head with frustration. "No, I'm not saying that. I'm saying if you love him, really love him, maybe you should start thinking about adoption. I realize it's harder for a single person to adopt a child, but it can be done. Jack and I will help you all we can and I'm sure Mom and Dad would, too."

"I'm not so sure of that," Sierra said doubtfully. "They probably think I should be more concerned about having children of my own."

"Sierra!" Gloria gently scolded. "You were always the sensible sister. But you're not thinking clearly now. Mom and Dad understand that Bowie has become a part of your life and they also understand that he needs a home as much as you want to give him one."

Sierra didn't realize her emotions were working over-time until she drew in a deep breath and her whole body trembled from the effort. "I'm so glad to hear you say that, Gloria. I thought maybe my family would try to discourage me. And I have been thinking about adoption. It's in the back of my mind all the time."

Smiling brightly, Gloria squeezed her hand. "Then why don't you go for it, girl? Bowie can grow up with his cousin." She patted her growing tummy. "And who knows, maybe Christina and Derek will decide to have a family soon and they'll be a threesome, just like their mothers."

Sierra studied her sister as all sorts of joyous and

doubtful thoughts mingled together to put a mixture of confusion on her face.

"I—I'm just not sure, Gloria. It's a big step. And I don't know—" She stopped as she realized she'd been about to say she didn't know what Alex might think of the whole thing. He was a part of her life now and she wanted him to remain a part of it. His feelings in the matter had to be considered. But it was too early to explain any of her concerns to Gloria, so she tried her best to smile. "I don't exactly know what sort of steps I'd need to take to be a candidate for adoption."

Gloria's smiled turned clever. "Darlin', your friend Alex is a lawyer. If you ask him, I'm sure he'd be glad to help."

Chapter Ten

Late that afternoon, Babies Unlimited sent a man out with the crib and matching dresser. Once he had the pieces of furniture in place and had driven away, Sierra quickly put the finishing touches to the room and closed the door. She didn't want Alex to get even a tiny glimpse of the new nursery. Not until she was ready to share it with him.

She'd kept the project a secret in hopes of surprising him. Now that it was completed, she couldn't wait for him to arrive home from work.

Alex finally arrived a little after six. She was in the bedroom changing out of the clothes she'd cooked supper in when she heard his footsteps heading toward the kitchen.

"In here, Alex," she called out to him.

Seconds later, he paused in the open doorway of their bedroom and gave a low whistle as he eyed her in a lacy red bra and matching panties.

"Hey, hey, hey. You don't need to dress for supper. You look fantastic like that."

He strode into the room, and, laughing, Sierra quickly stepped into a blue cotton shift and pulled it up over her hips.

"You can see through the kitchen curtains and we do have close neighbors, you know." As he approached her, she turned her back to him. "Would you zip me?"

"There's nothing in the world I'd rather do," he assured her, but before his hands pulled the folds of her dress together, he bent his head and pressed a kiss to the base of her neck. "Mmm. You smell delicious."

"That's steak," Sierra corrected him.

He chuckled and slid his arms around her waist and drew her backside against the front of his body. "No," he said against her cheek. "That's you."

"Losing your sense of smell along with your eyesight," she teased. "Pretty soon your sense of touch will be gone."

"If that's the case, I'd better make the most of what little time I have left," he murmured while running his hands up to her breasts and cupping his fingers around the small mounds.

"Oh, no." Sierra grabbed hold of his misbehaving hands and twisted around in his arms. "I've made a special supper for you and I don't want it getting cold."

Alex was just as happy to have the front of her shapely curves pressing into him and he slipped his hands to her buttocks and drew the juncture of her thighs tightly against his manhood.

"What could be more special than making love?" he wanted to know.

"Steak and baked potatoes and strawberry shortcake."

Alex shook his head. "Couldn't hold a light to you."

Sierra's soft laughter was playfully mocking. "You're a wicked, wicked guy, Alex Calloway." She slipped her arms around his neck and, rising on tiptoe, placed a soft kiss on his lips. His hand slipped into her hair and cradled the back of her head so that his lips continued to hover over hers. Sierra was almost tempted to tell him they'd forget supper.

"I'm dying to show you just how wicked," he whispered.

Woozy with desire, she inhaled deeply and turned her back to him. As she motioned for him to zip her dress, she said, "That naughty part of you is just going to have to wait until later tonight. I have a surprise for you."

"A surprise?" That got his attention and he quickly zipped her dress and fastened the hook and eye at the neckline. Then, smoothing his hands over her shoulders and down her arms, he said, "Don't tell me you've invited our friends over."

Her forehead puckered with a frown as she twisted her head around and looked up at him. "Why would I do that when our regular lunch get-together is tomorrow?"

Tomorrow? He'd forgotten all about it. Last week, the meeting had been canceled because Trey's job had taken him out of town and Mario had been tied up at the hospital. Since then too much had happened to think about meeting his friends at the Longhorn.

"Oh. I forgot. Are we going?"

Wide eyed, she turned to face him. "Well, why wouldn't we?" she countered with surprise. "They're our friends. They'll be worrying and wondering if we don't show up."

Alex shrugged and was surprised when he felt color springing to his cheeks. "I understand that. But it's going to be kind of different now. With us—well, you know—together."

"Why, Alex," she scolded gently. "Are you embarrassed to let them know that the two of us are close?"

"Uh, no." He dropped his hold on her and made a helpless gesture with his hands. "But they're probably going to think it's strange. Especially the part about Bowie. None of them have learned about you having the baby, much less about me."

She watched as he reached up and pulled the olive green printed tie from around his neck and tossed it onto the bed. As his fingers moved down the buttons of his shirt, his gaze slipped away from her and Sierra felt a tiny chill pass over her.

"Alex, are you—ashamed for them to know that you're with me?"

His green gaze flew back to hers. "Of course not!"

Uncertain, she stepped forward and curled her fingers

over his forearm. "Well, something's making you un-comfortable about seeing them. What is it?"

He shook his head, then rubbed the back of his neck. "You," he said. "I don't want any of them thinking badly of you. Your morals have always been high and I don't want them getting the idea that you've lowered them with me."

The notion was so sweet and old-fashioned that she had to smile at him. "Oh, Alex, we're not living in the dark ages. They're not going to label me a hussy just because you're sleeping by my side."

"They damn well better not," he growled. "If anyone insults you, they'll have to answer to me."

If he was that all-fired worried about her honor, why didn't he make an honest woman out of her? Sierra wanted to ask him. But there was no way she could get words like that past her lips. He'd probably run back-ward so fast, he'd hurt himself. And anyway, she wasn't so sure that marrying Alex would be the right step for her. Even though he spent most of his time with her right now, he was a bachelor at heart. Once he grew bored with her, he'd drift on to someone else. That was the way Alex had always worked.

"Thank you, Sir Galahad." She pecked a short kiss on his cheek then turned and walked to the door. "I'm going to finish supper. It'll be ready in five minutes, so hurry."

He looked over his shoulder at her with an expres-sion hovering between teasing and serious.

"I'm not hungry for food."

Sierra scraped a forefinger down the length of the opposite forefinger, but her chuckle softened the shameful gesture. "All you lawyers are the same. You have to win, at any cost."

Ten minutes later the two of them were sitting at the dining table eating the juicy steak that Sierra had broiled on the charcoal grill. Between bites, Alex began to tell her all about his day.

By the time they finished the strawberry shortcake he was telling jokes and laughing and Sierra was relieved to see him relaxed again. He had such a stressful job he didn't need silly worries about her piled on him, too.

"Okay, now what is this surprise you tempted me with? You said you went shopping today. Was it the lingerie department?" His eyes glinted devilishly. "Maybe something with a garter belt and fishnet hose?"

Her heart was suddenly beating very fast. Not because he'd suggested the two of them doing something erotic together. No, she was thinking about the nursery and whether he was going to view her work as a sign she wanted to keep Bowie on a permanent basis. There was no way she could know exactly how he felt about that prospect. Since the day he'd told child care services that the two of them were engaged and planning a family, he'd not talked about the future with Sierra. Not the far future. But then Alex had always been a person who lived from week to week and the only thing he took seriously was his work.

"Uh, no, sorry. It's nothing like that." Her smile was

hesitant as she released a nervous little laugh. "If you're finished eating, I'll show you."

"I couldn't eat another bite," he assured her.

Sierra rose from her chair and reached for his hand. "Okay. Close your eyes and I'll lead you."

He chuckled as he stood and obediently closed his eyes, then placed his hand in hers. Sierra's heart pounded with nervous anticipation as she led him to the door of the nursery and swung it wide.

"You can open your eyes now," she said.

She watched his eyelids flutter open and the faint amusement on his face instantly disappeared as surprise took over. He stared at the bright, happy wallpaper, the curtains, the chest and finally the crib with its colorful mobile of bugs and butterflies.

"What, uh, when did you do all of this?"

She followed him as he stepped into the room.

"I've been working on it all week. I didn't tell you because I wanted it to be a surprise."

He continued to look around the room as though he'd never seen a nursery before. "Well, you've certainly surprised me."

Sierra reached for his hand and twined her fingers through his. "Bowie deserves to have a real nursery. And I wanted it to look nice. I'll admit I paid a hefty amount for the crib and chest. But hopefully I'll be using it again, when I have more children."

Her last two words caught his attention and he arched a brow at her. "More children? Are you trying to tell me you're pregnant?"

Sierra could feel hot color consume her face. "Why, no. I told you I take an oral contraceptive."

"Pills can be forgotten," he said dryly.

His caustic remark hit Sierra hard, but she tried her best not to let it hurt her. Alex had always been frank and sarcastic at times. She'd decided a long time ago that you had to take the good with the bad if you wanted to hang around with Alex Calloway.

"I never forget," she said in a voice sharp enough to catch his attention.

He looked down at her and suddenly his features softened. "I didn't mean it that way, Sierra."

Still stinging from the insensitive comment, she said, "Just to ease your mind, I'd never trap a man that way. And that includes you, Alex Calloway."

Alex released a heavy sigh. He didn't know why he'd said such a thing to Sierra. In his heart he was certain she wasn't that type of woman. But the second he'd laid his eyes on the nursery he'd felt smothered and scared. Now she was probably thinking he was just using her.

Well, aren't you, Alex?

The inward voice stabbed him swift and deep. Was he using Sierra just for a sexual partner? No. She was more to him that that. But just how much more was a question he was afraid to answer.

"All right, honey." He slipped his arm around her shoulders and drew her to him. "I'm sorry. I know you're not like that. Forgive me, huh?"

It wasn't Sierra's nature to stay angry for more than

a minute or two and she grinned shyly up at him. "You're forgiven. Now tell me what you think about the nursery."

Once again his gaze swung full circle around the room. "You've obviously put a lot of work into it. And you've done a great job. If Bowie was old enough to really see it, I'm sure he'd be goo-gooing with pleasure."

She laughed softly. "Well, he will be gooing and squealing when he starts pulling up to the side of the crib and looking around at things."

Walking over to the baby bed, she pointed to the intricately carved posts. "See, the posts are close together so he can't get his little head hung between them. And these things around the bottom are bumper pads so when he starts rolling, he won't hurt himself. I looked at one of those portable intercom things, too. So that way if he makes even a tiny noise I could hear him. But they were rather pricey and I'd already spent so much on the furniture I decided I'd better wait until I get another paycheck."

"Always the practical woman," he murmured somewhat absently, then, rubbing his fingers across his forehead, he pulled his gaze away from the bed to look at her.

"What does this all mean, Sierra? I don't think you would have done all of this unless you have long-term plans for Bowie."

She drew in a long, bracing breath and released it. "I've been doing a lot of studying about that, Alex. And—" She paused as she pushed back a heavy swath of black hair from her shoulders and tried to find the right words. "I guess you can tell I'm crazy about Bowie."

He nodded. "I'd have to be blind not to see it."

"He—well, he feels like my boy. My own baby." Her brown eyes turned pleading as she looked up at him. "It's hard for me to explain just how I'm feeling. But all I can tell you is that I don't want to give him up."

He walked over to the crib and, with his forefinger, made an antenna on one of the butterflies bounce up and down. "Why should you have to give him up? I'm sure you can continue to be his foster mother until they find a good home for him."

Alex's green eyes were searching her face so intently that Sierra had to break eye contact and her gaze dropped to the blue-and-white checked comforter spread across the bottom of the crib.

Swinging her head back and forth, she said, "Who knows when or if Ginger might show up to reclaim him."

"You got that letter from her mother the other day. It should have reassured you that the Rollins family isn't going to stake any claims on the baby."

Her eyes darted up to his, then back to the comforter. "It did reassure me to a certain point. But I don't want to take any chances. I've decided I want to adopt Bowie."

He didn't say anything and suddenly the room was so quiet and tense Sierra was sure he could probably hear the loud beating of her heart.

"Adopt?"

The one-word question came out softly, as though he wasn't certain he'd heard correctly.

Sierra quickly closed the distance between them and wrapped her hand around his arm. "Yes, adopt. What do you think about it, Alex? Will you help me?"

"Help you?" His features twisted with comical disbelief. "You are kidding, aren't you?"

Sierra felt a cool wind wafting through the room. It slipped down her spine and sent goose bumps crawling up the backs of her arms.

"No. I wouldn't kid about something so serious. I'm asking you to help me."

Suddenly he turned his back to her, threw up his arms, then let them fall with a heavy whack against his sides. "What in hell are you thinking, Sierra? Asking me, of all people, to help you adopt?"

Stunned by the censure in his voice, Sierra stepped backward and swallowed hard. "I—you helped me gain foster care. I thought—I'd hoped you be happy to help make Bowie my baby. Don't you—care for him, even the least little bit?"

Her question seemed to insult and irritate him even more and through clenched teeth he let out a loud groan. "Damn it, Sierra! Of course I care for Bowie. That's not what this is about."

She looked at him, her eyes shadowed with pain and confusion. "It isn't?"

He whirled back to her. "No! It isn't! You're talking about *adoption*. That's a big step for anyone, much less a single woman."

"I realize that."

He frowned. "You're young, Sierra. You'll eventually have children of your own."

"I hope so. I want Bowie to have brothers and sisters. I'm sure you understand it's not good to grow up alone."

"And it's damn sure not good to grow up believing you're a real part of the family when you aren't!"

Like a cold rain, disappointment washed through her. "Oh. So that's where you're coming from," she said with regret. "Well, I'm sorry I asked for your help. But since you are a lawyer and my friend—my *closest* friend—you were my first choice."

Sierra didn't wait for him to respond. She brushed past him and walked out of the nursery. As she hurried toward the kitchen, tears burned her throat, but she refused to give in to them. Alex might think she was a pushover, but he was going to see just how tough she could be.

She was bending over the bassinet to make sure Bowie was still sleeping, when Alex came up behind her and wrapped his hand around her upper arm.

"Come here. We've got to talk."

The hurt part of her wanted to resist him. But the sensible side realized the two of them had to talk. She didn't want to remain at loggerheads with him. She loved him. She needed his arms around her. She needed his support.

"All right."

She allowed him to lead her into the living room

where the television was tuned in to the weather channel. Sierra didn't need to see the forecast. She could already predict a brewing storm.

Sierra sat down on the couch and expected him to join her. Instead he stood in front of her for a moment, quietly studying her face, and then he began to pace around the room until she got the impression she was on the witness stand and he was about to cut her to pieces.

After a moment, she said, "I thought you wanted to talk."

"I do. I'm trying to think of a way to make you understand that adopting Bowie is all wrong. For you. For me. For Bowie."

She tried not to flinch at his harsh words.

"Why?" she demanded. "How could loving and nourishing a child be wrong? Alex, I don't understand. You do have a heart and sometimes you even use it."

He stopped in the middle of the room and twisted his head in her direction. "This is not a time for sarcasm," he accused.

Her mouth popped open. "Then don't use any on me," she snapped.

He appeared to be taken aback by her sudden show of fire and Sierra watched him walk over and take a seat next to her.

"Listen, Sierra, none of this has anything to do with Bowie—"

"I beg your pardon?" she interrupted hotly. "It has *everything* to do with him!"

His hand came up before she could finish speaking.

"Just wait until I finish, please."

She glared and he continued, "I love Bowie. You might not think I'm capable of such an emotion, but I am. And, in the long run, I want what's best for the boy. He needs parents. Two of them. A nice married couple who will see that he's loved and cared for."

"I don't have to be married to give Bowie love and a good home," she shot back at him. "You and I both know that. Besides, I'm only twenty-eight. I don't plan on staying single for the rest of my life."

No quick retort came from his lips and Sierra realized her remark had taken their battle to dangerous ground.

His jaw like granite, he said, "Really. Is that what this is all about? You want the two of us to get married and adopt Bowie?"

She started to scream "No" out loud, but somehow managed to stop the word before it passed her lips. How could she answer no, when he'd just spoken her most fervent wish? Of course she'd imagined her and Alex married with Bowie and more children to go with him. It was a wonderful dream, even though, in the back of her mind, she understood it would never happen.

Her heart aching, she asked softly, "Would that be so bad?"

Cursing, he jumped to his feet. "Hell, yes! I don't want to be married. I don't want to have to trust anyone that much. And I sure as hell don't want to be the one who has to tell Bowie that somewhere out there he has two parents who didn't want him, who deserted him without a backward glance!"

Pushing herself to her feet, Sierra's lips quivered as she met his fierce gaze.

"Well, don't worry, Alex Calloway. Because I wouldn't marry you even if you got down on your belly and crawled across the floor to ask me!"

His nostrils flared with anger. "I wouldn't turn myself into a snake for any woman."

Sierra laughed scathingly. "Turn into? You already are one, Alex. Poison through and through."

Not waiting around to hear more, she held her head up and walked briskly to the kitchen and began to blindly gather up the remnants of their special meal.

Her plans to surprise Alex had backfired big time, she thought wretchedly. But at least now his feelings toward her and Bowie were crystal clear. There was nothing permanent about them.

She was scraping plates, hoping the simple task would stop her hands from trembling, when she heard footsteps behind her.

Turning, she saw Alex standing in the doorway. A grim look was on his face and slowly but surely she felt her insides dying. "Yes," she acknowledged.

"I've gotten my things loaded into the SUV. I'm leaving."

He might as well have punched her in the stomach with his fist. It wouldn't have hurt any more than his blunt farewell.

Wiping her hands on a dish towel, she walked toward him. "You're leaving?"

He nodded and she couldn't help notice that he was

avoiding eye contact. Maybe this wasn't any easier for him than it was for her, she thought.

"Well, I guess it's for the best," she said soberly. "There's no sense in us trying to be together when we're really worlds apart. And I—I'm sorry I said those nasty things to you, Alex. You have a right to feel as you do."

"I'm glad you understand that much," he said stiffly.

"Goodbye, Alex."

"Yeah," he muttered, then turned on his heel and hurried out of the room.

Just as Sierra heard the front door click behind him, Bowie started to squirm and cry. As Sierra picked the baby up from the bassinet, she cried along with him.

Chapter Eleven

Early the next morning, Sierra was giving Bowie a bath in the kitchen sink when the telephone rang.

Muttering with annoyance, she ignored the sound until she'd rinsed the baby and wrapped him in a towel. By then the caller had hung up so she laid Bowie on the table to diaper him. She'd just finished that task, when the phone began to shrill a second time.

Quickly she wrapped a thin blanket around Bowie and hurried over to the portable phone on the kitchen cabinet.

"Hello," she said with a hint of weary exasperation. She'd had one of those horrible nights where she'd not gotten a wink of sleep. With Alex's leaving, her insomnia had returned big time and she was totally drained from having no rest.

"Oh, you're there. I had just about decided you must already be at work."

Her heart sank when she heard her old college friend Gayle's voice on the other end of the line. Damn, damn. Today was the group's regular lunch day at the Longhorn. What was she going to do? She couldn't face Alex. Not today.

"Hi, Gayle. What's up?" she asked while desperately trying to keep her voice light and natural. Which was a major effort when her nasal passages were swollen from last night's flood of tears.

"Just calling to make sure you can make it to lunch today. And if you haven't eaten breakfast yet, then don't. I want you to try that fudge brownie dessert with me. Remember?"

A fattening dessert was the least of her worries, Sierra thought. "Uh—I don't know, Gayle. Something has come up."

"Are you sick?" the blonde quickly questioned.

"No, no. Nothing like that."

"Oh, then it's work." Gayle was quick to presume. "Sorry, Sierra. Can't you get away even for thirty minutes? I wanted to see how things have been going with you since old Chad headed for the hills."

Sierra nearly choked on something between a sob and a laugh. "Gayle—listen, I really don't think I can come to lunch today. And it's not my job that's causing the problem. Actually I'm on a short leave from work right now."

"Hmm. Must be nice being a lady of leisure," Gayle teased. "So what's the problem?"

"Alex."

There was a long pause, then Gayle said in a quiet, strained voice, "Oh?"

Sierra could imagine the other woman's red lips pursing with disapproval. "Yes. We—uh—had an argument. And I really don't want to sit across the table from him right now. If you know what I mean."

"Dear God. It must have been an awful one," Gayle exclaimed. "What happened? I saw you two together out in the parking lot talking after our last lunch. Is that when you argued?"

Bowie was eating his fist and beginning to put up a fuss for his bottle. In an attempt to pacify him, Sierra gently bounced him against her shoulder. "Gayle, it's a long story. And I really don't want to go into it over the phone."

By now Bowie was letting out a squall of impatience and naturally Gayle picked up on the sound.

"Sierra, do I hear a baby in your house?"

Sierra sighed. Maybe it would be good for her to meet with Gayle and get some of this awful weight off her shoulders, she thought. She'd always shared her personal life with the other woman, it shouldn't matter that Alex was their mutual friend. Talking to Gayle would be much easier than facing her mother or sisters right now. The last thing she wanted was for her family to find out she'd already lost another man.

Oh well, at least there was one good thing about Alex's leaving, Sierra thought glumly: she wouldn't have to do some heinous task for her sisters now.

"Yes. That's Bowie," she answered Gayle. "He's three weeks old and I'm a foster mother now."

"Sierra!" Gayle shrieked with surprise. "When did this come about? And why haven't you called me?"

Just like a waiting man, Bowie's patience had worn completely thin. His face was as red as a cowboy's bandana and he was screaming so loudly in Sierra's ear she could hardly decipher Gayle's words.

"Sorry, Gayle. I've got to get off the telephone. I'll meet you at the burger hut around twelve, okay?"

"Wild horses couldn't keep me away," Gayle assured her.

It *would* be raining, Alex thought grimly, as he pulled into the covered parking area of San Antonio International Airport. He didn't like to fly when it was raining, even in a big jet. But for the first time in ages, he'd managed to clear the weekend of work, and since he had nothing else to do, he'd decided to fly up to Dallas to see his parents. His father's birthday wasn't for another week, but he'd called and warned his mother that this would be the only time he could make it.

Inside the airport terminal, Alex waited until the last minute to go through security and board the plane. Later he was glad he'd not been too eager to get into the confines of the airliner. The flight was grounded for forty minutes due to lightning. A delay that was longer than the amount of time it took a jet to fly to Dallas.

To pass the time, Alex rested his head on the back of the seat and tried to sleep. He'd had a trying week at work with everything from taking on a client accused of murdering his wife, to thugs begging for his help to keep them out of prison, to a woman who wanted to sue her ex-husband because he'd taken her cat.

Who the hell was he kidding? Alex asked himself. He had that sort of stuff waltz in and out of his office every week. Normally he thrived on the chaos and even enjoyed Pauline's tirades. She gave him something to laugh about. But this week, his secretary had stretched his nerves to the breaking point and he'd ended up yelling at her every fifteen minutes.

He realized he was a temperamental man and he'd never understood how Pauline put up with him. But he was thankful that she did. He'd have to give her a raise or send her on some special cruise or something. His devoted secretary was irreplaceable and he didn't want to lose her.

Suddenly from somewhere behind him a baby's cry pierced the plane's interior.

Bowie!

Like a fool, he twisted around in his first-class seat to look. Several rows behind him, he spotted a woman holding a baby against her shoulder. The child was wearing tiny bib overalls and the woman was patting his back in an effort to soothe and quiet him.

The sight caused Alex's gut to clench with regret

and he jerked his head back to the front of the plane and tried to push the image out of his mind. Damn it, one of the reasons he'd come on this trip was to make an effort to get Sierra and Bowie out of his mind. But he should have known that was stupid, wishful thinking. Everywhere, everything reminded him of the two of them.

The past week had been more awful than he could have ever imagined. He'd never felt pain like this in his whole life. Not even when he'd found his adoption papers and he'd discovered the truth of his birth.

The night Alex had walked out of Sierra's house, he'd never expected to feel the sort of misery that was now weighing him down. He'd expected to feel a bit glum for a day or two, then his head would clear and he'd realize he was relieved to be disentangled from the family situation he'd created by being with Sierra.

Unfortunately it hadn't worked the way he'd expected. So far, he'd never experienced anything remotely related to relief. He ached to see Sierra. He wanted to hold her, make love with her, the way they'd made love before. He wanted to see little Bowie, hold the baby against his chest and kiss his smooth cheek.

"Sir?"

A hand touched his shoulder and he looked up to see a young woman with curly black hair bending over him. For a split second Sierra's face swam in front of his vision.

"Sir, I'm sorry to disturb you. Would you like something to drink once we get in the air? A soda, water, a bourbon and Coke, perhaps?"

Alex mentally shook himself and looked up at the flight attendant. She was a young beauty with a wide smile and blue eyes that were twinkling brightly back at him. Any other time, he would have been taking advantage of the situation. But today the woman didn't spark even a tiny interest in him. He felt dead and empty inside and he was smart enough to know that the void couldn't be filled by just a pretty face.

"No, thanks," he told her. "But could you tell me when we might be taking off?"

"I believe the weather system is almost past us now, sir. We should be taking off shortly."

She moved on down the aisle of passengers and Alex let out a heavy sigh. No doubt about it, he thought grimly. He was a ruined man.

Two hours later, Alex's flight set down at Dallas-Fort Worth International. Since he only had a carry-on bag, he walked straight to the outer terminal and began to search through the crowd for his parents. The two of them had insisted on picking Alex up at the airport instead of allowing him to take a taxi to their home in north Dallas.

Thankfully he spotted his mother rather quickly and called to her over the heads of several rambunctious boys pushing and fighting their way toward the next terminal.

Where were the little heathens' parents? he wondered. Never, under any circumstance, would he allow Bowie to behave so wildly in public.

Don't worry, Alex. It's not going to be up to you to

see that Bowie is taught manners and respect. Some other man will come into Sierra's life and help her guide the little boy into manhood.

"Alex!" his mother shouted excitedly.

She started toward him and Alex increased his long strides to pass the rowdy boys and meet up with his mother.

"Hi, Mom. You look great." He hugged her close and kissed her cheek and she beamed up at him with a joy that left him somehow ashamed of himself.

"Gosh, it's so good to see you, son." She kissed him back, then turned to her husband who'd stepped up behind the two of them. "Doesn't he look wonderful, darlin'?"

A wide smile split Mitch Calloway's face as he stepped forward and reached for his son's hand. With a firm grip, Alex shook his father's hand. Then, at the last moment, before he released his hold, something made Alex move even closer and give his dad a hug.

"Nice to see you, Dad."

Mitch, a tall, ruggedly built man with iron-gray hair, patted Alex's shoulder with obvious affection. "It's wonderful to have you home for a few days, son."

The older man's gaze left Alex to look at his wife and even though a word wasn't spoken between the two of them, Alex could see they were silently communicating, the way couples did after they'd been together for many, many years. And they were both expressing their surprise over Alex's warm greeting.

The whole idea left Alex feeling a little awkward

and he reached down and picked up the leather bag sitting next to his feet.

"Well, if you two are ready, let's get out of here," he suggested. "This has been a heck of a flight."

"We were beginning to get worried," Emily said as the three of them headed toward the nearest exit. "Especially after we heard the flight was delayed due to thunderstorms. I don't even trust these planes in dry weather, much less in a storm."

"Well, he's here safe and sound now, dear. You can quit chewing your nails," Mitch teased.

Emily laughed as she looped her arm through Alex's. "Your dad is trying to be amusing," she said to Alex. "He knows I couldn't chew these acrylic things even if I had beaver teeth."

Alex's mother was always graciously dressed in feminine clothing and her hair, makeup and nails groomed to a tee. She was the epitome of a Dallas lady and Alex couldn't help thinking how different she and Sierra were in their outward appearances, but how alike they were in matters of the heart. They were both loving, caring women who put the needs of others before their own. How many men in the world were lucky enough to be loved by women like that? he wondered.

Whoa, Alex. You don't know that Sierra ever loved you. She made love with you. But that could have been just sex. And even if it had been love, you blew it. You showed her what a selfish bastard you really are.

Thankfully his mother began to chatter and Alex was forced to thrust the miserable thoughts from his mind as best he could. But later, as he and his parents drove to the Calloway home, the accusing little voice inside him kept coming back again and again.

Two days later, on Sunday morning, Sierra took Bowie and herself to early mass, then drove out to her parents' home for breakfast. She'd not seen any of her family since Alex had moved out and dread was boiling in the pit of her stomach. Even though she doubted any of them was aware how much she and Alex had shared those two weeks, she knew that her mother had her mind set on the two of them getting together romantically.

That idea was enough to make her groan out loud. If her mother only knew just how close she'd been with Alex, she'd be shocked. Or would she? Her mother wasn't a prude. She understood what it was like to love a man with all your heart. And that was the way she loved Alex. She might as well face the dismal fact.

When Sierra walked into her parents' kitchen, she was surprised to find her two sisters sitting at the breakfast table. Both Gloria and Christina got up from their chairs to greet her with a hug and a kiss.

"Let me hold Bowie," Gloria said, already reaching to take the baby from Sierra's arms. "My, my, he's growing in leaps and bounds. And he's so bright eyed. I think he's actually picking up our images."

"He's probably picking up all that cackling you girls are doing," Jose teased from the end of the table where he was trying to read the Sunday morning paper.

"Oh, Daddy, that's awful," Christina scolded him. "Your daughters have always been quiet and refined."

As Gloria took a seat with Bowie carefully cradled in her arms, Jose eased down his paper and laughed.

"Quiet and refined? Honey," he called to his wife. "Do you hear your daughter? Maybe we should bring out some of the old home videos."

Maria approached the table with a platter of chorizo sausage and eggs. As she placed it next to a stack of warm tortillas, she said, "Jose, if we let them see what a handful they were to raise we might never get grand-children. Just let them keep on thinking they were quiet, obedient girls."

Except for Sierra, everyone around the table laughed. But she wasn't in the mood for laughter. She'd hoped that being with her family would lift her spirits. She'd thought the visit might actually help rid her heart of the misery she felt over Alex. But being here with her parents and siblings was only reminding her of all that she'd lost when he'd walked out the door.

Picking up Bowie's diaper bag, she headed to the cabinet counter. "If we're ready to eat," Sierra said, "I'd better heat up Bowie's formula. I don't think he's up to chorizo yet."

"Oh, yes, Sierra, and let me feed him," Gloria called over to her. "I need the practice. And he needs to eat more than I do."

Christina shook a finger at her sister. "Gloria, when are you going to remember that you're eating for two? You can't have a healthy baby eating like a bird."

"A bird," Gloria said with a laugh. "I've gained five

pounds already! You just want me to look like a sow at my wedding, so that you'll be the most beautiful bride when your wedding comes around."

Christina groaned with amused disbelief. "Bologna! Derek and I will probably wind up eloping. Planning a big, grand wedding is such a bother."

Maria stared openmouthed at Christina while Gloria laughed loudly.

"Oh, sure, Christina, that's the biggest whopper you've ever told."

Sierra glanced over at the two of them just in time to see Gloria patting her thickening stomach and Christina giggling with amusement.

A pang of envy hit Sierra hard. But on the other hand, she could acknowledge that she was happy her sisters had found love and happiness. Maybe the same sort of joy would come to her someday. But she couldn't imagine loving anyone other than Alex. So where did that leave her? Single for the rest of her life?

With everyone lingering around the table to finish their coffee, breakfast lasted more than an hour. Sometime during the meal, Bowie fell asleep in Gloria's arms and she carried the child to the couch and carefully covered him with a light blanket before she returned to her seat next to Sierra.

Eventually Jose announced he'd had enough female conversation to last him awhile. He left the table and went outside to get the riding lawn mower out of the garage.

As soon as the door closed behind him, Maria turned a worried look on her youngest daughter. "All right, my little one, now that your father is out of hearing range, what is wrong with you this morning? We haven't seen or heard from you in days and now that you're here you act like the world is coming to an end."

Her world had come to an end, Sierra thought sadly. Maybe the sooner she admitted her fate the sooner she could accept it.

"I don't know why you think there's anything wrong. Daddy didn't."

Maria pursed her lips as she tore off a piece of flour tortilla. "There are some things that fathers just can't read in their daughters. And I didn't bring this up in front of him because I knew it would worry him to think you're having some sort of trouble."

Sierra studied her half-eaten breakfast while wondering if she was really that transparent or if her mother was the only one who could see the pain tearing through every part of her.

"There's no trouble, Mom," she did her best to deny. "I'm just a little wrung out from caring for Bowie. And I've been having more insomnia lately."

Maria was hardly convinced. "You've always suffered from insomnia, Sierra. And a few minutes ago, you told us Bowie was a wonderful baby. You said he rarely cried unless he was hungry and that he woke up only once during the night. It doesn't sound to me like he should have you all wrung out. Maybe you should go to the doctor and see why you're feeling so tired."

Sierra sipped at the last of her coffee. "I don't need a doctor, Mom. I'm fine. Just fine."

Her voice was so brittle the sound of it caused both her sisters to stare at her.

"Sierra!" Gloria gasped.

Christina leaned toward her youngest sister and placed a concerned hand on her shoulder. "Honey, what's the matter? Are you sick of hearing about Gloria and me getting married? Does that bother you?"

Feeling awful, Sierra bent her head and pinched the bridge of her nose. "No—it's nothing like that. I'm happy for you two. Really—very happy."

In spite of Sierra's struggle to appear normal, her voice broke on her last words, causing the other three women to exchange worried glances.

"All right," Maria spoke up firmly. "This is not like you, Sierra. Tell us what's happened. Is it Bowie? Is someone trying to take him away from you? The mother?"

Shaking her head fervently, Sierra lifted her head and sniffed at the tears threatening to pool in her brown eyes. "No. Nothing like that has happened. At least not yet."

"You're expecting it to?" Gloria spoke up.

Sierra looked at her. "Maybe. Hopefully not. I can't be certain, though."

"Dear God," Christina said softly, "that's enough to make you a nervous wreck."

"Yes. But—" Knowing she couldn't keep the truth from her family any longer, she paused to draw in a deep, bracing breath. "That's not the thing that has me so—miserable. It's Alex. He's—he's broken my heart."

Chapter Twelve

Maria grimly jerked her head up and down while Christina and Gloria looked at each other with arched brows.

"You've had an argument?" Maria questioned.

Sierra choked on a sob. "No, Mom. It's worse than that." Before she could change her mind, she began to blurt out everything from Alex staying with her, to how she'd fallen in love with him, to their argument, and finally his leaving.

By the time she was finished, her mother was quietly crying while her two sisters were ranting and raving about no-good men.

"Sierra, this is awful," Maria said with a sad sniff.

"So awful. I had hoped that you and Alex were going to get together. You seem so right for each other."

Sighing heavily, Sierra got up from her chair, carried her plate to the kitchen sink and began to wash the dishes that were already piled there. She had to move her body, to do something or else she was sure she was going to break right down the middle.

"Yes, I thought so, too, Mom. But it wasn't meant to be. Alex doesn't want to be a family man and it would be wrong of me to try to turn him into one."

"But he must care about Bowie," Maria reasoned. "Why would he be so against you adopting him?"

Sierra scrubbed at a tiny spot of dried egg on the edge of a plate. "He's adopted himself, Mom. Remember?"

"Yes," Christina spoke up. "I remember you talking about him once. You said he felt very bitter about his parents keeping the truth from him and you were trying to encourage him to forgive them."

Sierra nodded. "That was a long time ago. And I believe, for the most part, that he has forgiven his parents. But he doesn't want to have to be the one to tell Bowie that his real parents deserted him."

Gloria cast a worried look at her younger sister. "Maybe he believes Bowie would grow up to resent the two of you like Alex did his own parents?"

Pausing with her hands in the dishwater, Sierra stared thoughtfully out the window over the kitchen sink. Her father was going back and forth on the lawn tractor and enjoying every second of it. Even though Jose was a brilliant businessman, he was a deep family man. From all that her mother had told her, he had looked forward to having children and once she and her sisters had been born, he'd embraced the three of them with all his heart. If only Alex had those same traits, she thought wistfully. Perhaps then he wouldn't have been able to turn his back on her and Bowie. But she had to remember that her father had loved her mother from the very beginning and that was the key. Alex didn't love her. He'd only wanted her, desired her.

"I don't know," she mumbled. "It doesn't matter anyway. I'm going to forget about Alex Calloway. I'm going to concentrate on adopting Bowie. And as for Alex, he can go jump in the river."

Leaving her seat at the table, Christina walked over and put her arm around Sierra's slender shoulders. "Honey," she said in a voice only for Sierra's ears, "do you remember when I was going through that horrible sexual harassment case?"

"Of course I remember it," Sierra spoke quietly. "You went through hell at that time. Nobody believed you."

"Except for you," Christina said with affection. "You believed in me and you wouldn't let me give up. So I'm not going to allow you to give up and turn into a sob sister. If you love Alex, you'd better go after him. Make him see that the three of you are meant to be a family."

Sierra looked up from the sudsy water and stared at her sister through teary eyes. "Alex has always said I'm too soft. Maybe I should show him I'm not a complete marshmallow."

"Now you're talking, sweetie," Christina said, then

happily turned to Gloria and their mother. "Relax, you two, I've made her see reason. She's gonna fight for her man!"

"It's about time," Gloria muttered.

"Thank you God," Maria said reverently as she crossed herself. "Rosita's dream will come true now."

Sierra understood what dream her mother was talking about, but she didn't bother to point out that Rosita's dreams were just that—dreams. And Alex wasn't a marrying man.

Later that afternoon in Dallas, Alex was in his parents' backyard putting golf balls into a tin cup his father had sunk into the ground. He'd never been one to play the game in earnest, mainly because he was too busy trying to keep the electric bill paid at the office so that Pauline wouldn't have to resort to a hand fan. But his father loved the game and he enjoyed showing off his putting skills to Alex.

"Hey, you can't make that," Alex challenged good-naturedly as he watched his father place the ball about eighteen feet from the hole.

Across the yard, reclining on a lounger, Emily glanced up from the paperback book she was reading. The day was sunny and hot and his mother was wearing a pair of black capri pants with a matching shirt and a pair of white sunglasses with rhinestones dotting the rims. She looked like something out of a James Bond movie and Alex realized that next to Sierra his mother was the most beautiful and caring woman on earth. Why had it taken him this long to realize that?

"Don't bet on it, Alex," Emily said. "He does this for hours every day. He's an expert."

Mitch took his time lining up the shot and eventually gave the ball a solid nudge with his putter. To Alex's amazement the ball rattled around the lip of the hole, then fell in, and he laughed as his father pumped a triumphant fist in the air.

"I'm glad I didn't bet. You're getting salty, Dad. I won't be challenging you to eighteen holes anytime soon."

Smiling at the two of them, Emily tossed her book aside and stood up. "I'm going in to make iced tea," she announced. "You two want a glass?"

"Sure. Bring the pitcher," Alex answered.

Once his mother had disappeared into the house, Alex walked over to his father. "Dad, can I talk to you a minute?"

Picking up the seriousness in his voice, Mitch laid his putter aside and motioned for Alex to sit beside him on the porch steps where a sycamore dappled them with cooling shade.

"Let 'er rip," he invited.

As he looked into his father's strong face, Alex was suddenly overcome with emotions he'd never expected to feel.

"I—this is going to sound strange to you probably. But I—" He paused and shook his head in a helpless gesture. "Have you and Mother always been glad that you adopted me?"

Mitch's whole forehead jerked upward with surprise.

Then he studied his son's solemn face for long moments before he finally broke into a wide smile.

"We've always been very glad and very proud that you're our son. You don't doubt that, do you?"

At one time he had, Alex thought. Back when he was an impressionable, moody teenager he'd had this idea that Mitch and Emily had adopted him just so they could say they had a child like the rest of their friends. Not because they *loved* him. And later, well, he'd dwelled on the fact that they'd kept his adoption a secret rather than concentrate on all the wonderful things they'd done for him.

"No. I don't doubt it. But was there ever a time, in the very beginning, that you weren't sure about taking on a son who wasn't conceived from your genes?"

Mitch thoughtfully rubbed his chin. "Alex, I'll be honest with you. There were moments, before we ever signed the adoption papers, that I worried. Raising a child is a huge responsibility. I kept wondering if I could do it right. I asked myself what would happen if I couldn't take care of you financially. What if I suddenly died and left your mother with a baby to rear on her own. All sorts of questions like that ran through my head. But I never worried about your blood or your genes. I don't care about any of that," he argued gently. "The bond between us is what makes us father and son."

Until this moment Alex hadn't realized how closed off his heart had been. Now he could feel a heavy door slowly creaking open and a warm light flooding him.

"I'm lucky to have you, Dad. You and Mom both."

Mitch squeezed his shoulder and looked out across the manicured lawn. "Was there some reason you were thinking about all of this, Alex? All weekend I've gotten the sense that your mind has been occupied with something."

Alex nodded glumly. "There's this woman—I've known her for a long time and I care about her. She's—she's caring for a newborn who she wants to adopt. I told her she should wait and have children of her own. We ended up arguing bitterly—and I walked out."

"Why?" Mitch asked.

Alex sighed. "Because I'm a selfish bastard, I guess. Walking is easier than facing a woman with tears in her eyes."

"No. I mean why did you oppose her adopting the baby?"

Alex shrugged. Now that his father put the question to him point-blank, his reasons seemed foolish and selfish. "I don't really know. I just kept thinking that someday I'd have to tell him that his real parents hadn't wanted him. And I couldn't imagine having to see his pain."

Mitch gave his son's shoulder another encouraging squeeze. "The love you'll give him will make up for all of that. Don't you agree?"

Alex had to think only for a second before a slow smile began to spread across his face. "Yeah. I agree."

"So what are you going to do about this young woman?" Mitch asked.

The smile fell from Alex's face. "I don't know, Dad. I said some pretty awful things to her."

"I've said some pretty awful things to your mother, too. But thankfully for us men, most women are forgiving creatures."

"I can only hope," Alex told him.

Monday afternoon Sierra dressed carefully in a flirty knee-length skirt and a matching blouse. She secured the left side of her hair behind her ear with a pearl studded comb and allowed the rest to fall in curls around her shoulders.

Once she had finished with her makeup and gathered up Bowie and his diaper bag, she left the house and drove straight to the Stocking Stitch, her mother's knitting store in downtown Red Rock.

Upon hearing Sierra's plans to drive to San Antonio to see Alex at his law office, Maria had insisted on keeping Bowie while she made the trip. At first, Sierra was reluctant to leave the baby with her mother. She'd intended for Bowie to be with her when she faced Alex again. After all, the baby had been at the center of their argument and she wanted him to see that Bowie was still a part of her life. But her mother had finally convinced her that she needed to talk to Alex without the distraction of a baby.

As Sierra drove the twenty miles to San Antonio, she wasn't sure her mother was right about leaving Bowie with her. But then it probably wouldn't matter if the baby was right in front of Alex or back in Red Rock; she expected the man to be a hard case.

A half hour later, Sierra entered the front door of Calloway Law Office. No clients were seated in the small waiting area and Pauline was two-stepping around the room with a feather duster while on the radio George Strait was singing about coming unwound.

"Oh, Sierra. I didn't realize anyone had come in," she said the moment she spotted Sierra standing just inside the doorway.

The woman hurried over to the radio and turned down the volume. "Sorry about that," she said as she wiped her hands against the hips of her black slacks. "Alex is out and I'm all caught up on paperwork. And since I double as janitor, too, I thought it would be a good time to stir up some dust around here."

Sierra looked around the long, wood-paneled room. It was filled with a couch, several wooden hardback chairs, two lamps and three magazine racks. In one corner, a small television was tuned in to a soap opera, but the sound was turned off.

"Alex doesn't deserve you, you know," Sierra told her. "You should tell him that you don't do windows."

Pauline laughed. "I don't mind. Gives me a little exercise. Besides, I feel the same way as Alex. I don't want some stranger coming in here sniffing around our private papers and things. You can't trust anyone these days."

She motioned for Sierra to follow her over to the couch. "So I'm guessing you're here to see Alex." The woman sank onto the end cushion and crossed her legs out in front of her.

Sierra continued to stand. Now that she'd learned Alex was out, there wasn't any need for her to stay. She might as well get on back to the Stocking Stitch and relieve her mother of Bowie.

"I—was hoping to talk to him. I just took a chance that he'd be in." She hadn't wanted to call before making the drive over. She hadn't wanted to give Alex the chance to snub her without facing her first.

"That's too bad. He had opening arguments on an insurance fraud case today. And Judge Brookings is on the bench for this one. The old judge doesn't want to waste a minute of the taxpayers' money. If there's a spare half hour left in the day, he'll try to run two or three witnesses through examination."

Disappointment swamped Sierra. She'd gotten herself all psyched up for this meeting. Now she felt deflated.

"Oh. Well, I'll try to catch him later," she said to the secretary.

Sierra started toward the door and Pauline jumped up to follow her.

"Uh, you wouldn't happen to know what's been wrong with Alex, would you?" she asked. "He's turned into a regular monster. I think he's sick, but he refuses to go to the doctor."

Sierra shook her head. She hoped the other woman was wrong. To even think of Alex being ill caused her stomach to clench with alarm.

"No. I haven't seen Alex in…a few days," she said.

Pauline released a wistful sigh. "Well, at least he seemed better today. I guess spending the weekend with his parents helped him."

Sierra looked at her. "Alex went to Dallas?"

Pauline nodded. "Yes. Surprised the heck out of me. He doesn't go up there too often."

This news sent Sierra's head spinning and she replied in an absent voice, "No. He doesn't."

"Should I tell him you stopped by?" Pauline asked as Sierra reached to push open the door.

"Uh, no," Sierra answered. "Whenever I see him, I want it to be a surprise."

She said goodbye to Alex's secretary then stepped out into the late-evening sun. A humid breeze was blowing directly from the south and it fluttered the hem of Sierra's skirt and tossed the black curls around her head as she walked down the sidewalk toward her parked car.

She was trying to tell herself not to feel dejected when she heard someone calling her name. Turning, she was suddenly frozen by the sight of Alex hurrying down the sidewalk in her direction.

"Sierra, what are you doing here?"

His tie was loosened, the sleeves of his white shirt rolled back against his forearms and his brown hair windblown against his forehead. His muscular body appeared thinner through the midsection, his face gaunt and tired. Sierra suddenly wanted to burst into tears at the sight of him.

"I came by to see you."

She could see that her answer had shocked him. It was clear in the way his brows lifted and his green eyes widened ever so slightly. But after a moment he appeared to collect himself and he glanced over her shoulder toward her parked car.

"You don't have Bowie with you?"

She shook her head and his expression instantly turned fearful.

"What—you haven't done anything, have you? I mean, Bowie is still with you, isn't he?"

She wanted to ask him why it mattered to him, but she kept the sharp words buried inside of her. At least they were talking. That was better than what had transpired between them these past several days.

"Why, yes. My mother has him at the Stocking Stitch. Showing him off to all her knitting customers, I'm sure."

He let out a sigh of relief, then glanced thoughtfully down the sidewalk in the direction of his office. "Uh, come on," he told her. "Let's go back to the office. We can talk there."

His hand closed around her upper arm and Sierra's heart began to trip over itself. To have him touching her again was so exciting and familiarly sweet. No man had ever made her feel as Alex did and she was absolutely certain no man ever would.

They strode down the sidewalk and entered the law office. Alex quickly caught Pauline's attention and jerked his thumb toward the door. "Go home," he ordered.

Jumping to her feet, the secretary pulled her purse from a desk drawer and shoved her chair in place. "You don't have to tell me twice. But what happened with Brookings? I thought you'd be gone 'til six tonight."

Alex grinned slyly. "Brookings got mad at the A.D.A. for not turning over a piece of evidence to me.

Called us both in chambers and said he was fed up and for us to go home and come back in the morning."

Pauline laughed. "So now you have the judge in your pocket. I wish I had your charm, Alex Calloway."

She slipped out the door and Alex, who was still holding on to Sierra's arm, dropped it long enough to lock the door behind his secretary. Once he'd finished that task, he led Sierra to his private office.

After he'd closed the door, he took both her hands and led her over to his desk where a banker's lamp was still burning in the shadowy room.

"You look beautiful, Sierra," he said softly. "Do you know how happy I am to see you?"

Fear and pain and hope all coiled together inside of Sierra until all she could do was shake her head. "I—I haven't seen or heard from you in days…weeks now. How can I believe that you're happy to see me?" she asked doubtfully.

A frown quirked the muscles around his mouth as his hands released hers and began to slide seductively up her arms. "Maybe showing you would be better," he said huskily.

He leaned in to kiss her, but Sierra held him off, placing both hands against his chest. "No! None of that right now, Alex. We'd wind up right over there on your couch. And that wouldn't get us anywhere."

As far as Alex was concerned, it would get them everywhere. But he could see from the set of her jaw that she was resolute and the last thing he wanted to do was anger her more than he already had.

"All right," he gently agreed, but his concession didn't stop him from taking a firm hold on her hands once again. "I'm glad to see you because I want to apologize, Sierra. I was wrong. Flat wrong. And I'm asking you to forgive me."

Alex was apologizing to her? Sierra was shocked. It was a rare thing for the man to apologize to anyone, much less her. He usually considered a wink and a pat on the cheek a sufficient apology.

"Forgive you for what?" she asked. "Being a jackass?"

Alex tried not to outwardly flinch. "Honey, I—" He paused long enough to shake his head, then tried again. "Yeah, I guess I was a jackass. But I'm not anymore."

Her chin tilted to a challenging angle. "You've changed overnight?"

His little dove had turned into a tigress, Alex couldn't help thinking, as he studied the fiery sparks in her brown eyes. "Sort of. I don't know. Oh, hell, Sierra, don't keep me in misery. Are you going to forgive me or not?"

She studied him beneath dipped lashes. "What will it mean if I do?"

With a groan of misery, Alex reached out and brushed his knuckles against her throat and down the rosy-tan skin exposed by the deep V of her blouse.

"It means, my darlin', that the three of us will be together again. The way we should have been all along."

She released a shaky breath and Alex decided he couldn't keep his distance any longer. Slipping his arms around her waist, he pulled her close against him. The scent of lilac drifted up from her windblown hair.

"Alex, you've got to understand right now that I still have plans to adopt Bowie. With or without your help."

"I'm glad."

Disbelief swam across her face as she tilted her head back to look at him. "Glad? You said it was the wrong thing to do! What's happened to you Alex?"

Lifting his hands to her hair, he threaded his fingers through the silky strands until he was cradling the back of her head.

"I went to see my parents."

"Yes, Pauline told me. But you've gone to see your parents before. What has that got to do with you and me and Bowie?"

He smiled because he was a different man now and he desperately wanted her to understand that. "Because this visit was different, Sierra. When I first caught sight of my parents waiting for me at the terminal gate—I don't know—everything inside of me seemed to turn upside down. I was seeing my parents in a totally different light. I suddenly wanted to hug them close, to talk with them, listen to them, just be with them in a way I'd never wanted before. Does that make sense?"

Somewhere deep inside Sierra, a tiny flicker of hope tried to flare to life. "Yes. It does make sense. But why? Why now after all these years? There's been so many times that I've urged you to be thankful for your wonderful parents."

The smile on his face broadened even more and Sierra could only stare at him in wonder.

"I know. They are great, aren't they?"

"I'm glad you've finally realized that. But—"

"Don't you see, Sierra?" he interrupted. "It's because of you and Bowie. Being with you two, as a family, opened my eyes in a way I'd never expected."

"And when were you going to let me in on this change?" she asked accusingly. "I haven't heard from you since you walked out!"

Groaning with regret, he pulled her close. "You probably won't believe it, but I was planning to drive over to your place tonight, after court had recessed for the day." His gaze roamed adoringly over her face. "I couldn't believe my eyes a few minutes ago when I spotted you on the sidewalk. I—I was afraid you'd never speak to me again. The last thing I expected was for you to come here to me!"

"Alex—" She paused, her face marred with doubt as she looked at him. "Are you trying to tell me that you want to help me adopt Bowie now?"

He chuckled softly as his hands roamed her back and crushed her up against his hard body. "I'm trying to tell you that I want to marry you. I want for *us* to adopt Bowie."

Chapter Thirteen

"Marry you?" Sierra asked, shocked.

Alex grinned down at her. "That's what I said. I think we should get married. Don't you?"

This was not the sort of marriage proposal Sierra had dreamed of. She'd always pictured a ring, and maybe roses or lilies. Much more important, she'd believed she would be listening as the man in her life to be vowed his love and devotion. But love had never been mentioned.

Alex had never been bashful about speaking his mind. Getting the point across was his job. Knowing that, Sierra could only assume his feelings didn't include love.

"I—don't know, Alex," she said hesitantly. "Marriage is a huge step."

He studied her face for long seconds. "You don't want to marry me?"

She tried to breathe as a ball of emotion threatened to burst her heart. "I didn't say that."

He frowned. "Well, you sure don't seem to be cottoning to the idea."

She couldn't think rationally when he was holding her close. Not when every inch of her body was begging her to snuggle against him, to seek his kiss.

Pulling out of his embrace, Sierra turned and walked across the room. With her back to him, she said, "It's not that, Alex. You've shocked me. I don't know what to think."

"You don't believe I've changed. Is that it?"

Turning, she looked at him and instantly wished she hadn't. Just the sight of him was enough to remind her of all those nights they'd made love, all those mornings she'd woken in his arms.

"If you've changed your mind about adopting Bowie, then *you* must have changed."

He left the desk to stride quickly toward her and in that moment Sierra thought that she'd never seen him look so serious or so humble.

"I have changed, Sierra. I realized that all these years I didn't really resent my parents. Somewhere in the deepest part of me I knew that they loved me. I—well, all that anger I'd harbored was really directed at the man and woman who'd chosen to give me away, as if I were just a thing they didn't want."

Sierra felt as if her heart was tearing right down the

middle. How awful that he'd lived all this time with that sort of pain, she thought.

Closing the space between them, she touched his face, then stepped into his arms. "Oh, Alex, I've missed you so much. It's been awful since you left. I never want to go through that again."

Relief poured through Alex and he closed his eyes as he stroked her hair. "I haven't been able to eat or sleep or work. All I could think about was you and Bowie." He slipped his thumbs beneath her jaw and tilted her face up to his. "I never want to go through that much misery again, either. I want us to be married. I want Bowie to be ours and the three of us to be a family again."

Sierra wanted that, too. Desperately. But he didn't love her. He cared about her, but he wasn't in love with her. Could she live with that?

"Alex, maybe we should go slow and think—"

"Slow! Bowie is growing up even as we speak. If we file adoption papers, we need to be married. Sierra, you know that much without me having to tell you."

She drew in a long, shaky breath and let it out. "Alex, marriage is very serious. We haven't been a couple for very long. We need to know—"

He gave her a placating smile as he bent his head and touched his lips to her forehead. "Sierra, darlin', we've been friends, close friends, for nine years. We know more about each other than most couples that go through long engagements. Our marriage will work, honey. We'll make it work."

And she had to believe that, Sierra thought. Because, sensible or not, she had to have this man beside her.

"All right," she said with a little hesitant smile. "What sort of wedding date are you wanting?"

"Uh, how about tomorrow?" he asked quickly.

"You're not serious! We can't. I want to be married in church. Like my sisters."

"Dear Lord, Sierra, your sisters are planning huge, expensive ceremonies! Do you need all that to feel married to me?"

In her heart she already felt married to him and she clasped her hands around his. "I don't mean I want a fancy ceremony like that. I just don't want to settle for a quick exchange in the judge's chambers. I want the priest to pray over us."

"And so do I, Sierra. But we can do that in a week's time, can't we?"

"A week!" His suggestion was so wild that excitement began to pour through her and she began to laugh. "I'll have to put my sisters to work on this!"

Laughing with her, he bent his head and kissed her. "Let's go get our baby," he whispered.

The next morning after a bite of breakfast, Sierra made a beeline to San Antonio and dropped Bowie off with the good sisters at St. Anthony's child care services. Since Gloria had learned she was expecting, she'd already made a point of searching out reputable day cares and she'd suggested to Sierra that she might want to use St. Anthony's once she started back to work. And with that time being only two weeks away, Sierra figured today would be a good time to give Bowie a chance to get adjusted.

Once she'd made sure the baby was safely settled and content, she drove straight to Gloria's jewelry shop, the Love Affair. When Sierra entered the building, there were already two customers inside perusing her sister's beautiful creations.

Sierra waited by one of the glass counters while Gloria waited on the two patrons. Eventually they both made purchases and left the shop. By then Sierra was about to burst with her news.

"Sierra! What are you doing out so early? And where's my sweet Bowie?"

Sierra cast her sister a sly smile. "He's at St. Anthony's. And I'm here in the city to do a bit of clothes shopping."

Gloria giggled. "You, clothes shopping? This is a first. You've never been into fashion. What's brought this on?"

Sierra couldn't hold it in any longer; a bubbly laugh burst past her lips. "I'm getting married! This coming Saturday! I need a dress, and fast. Will you help me find one?"

"Married! Next Saturday!" Gloria was clearly shocked and she hurried around the glass showcases to take Sierra by the hand. "Sierra, are you—did you take something that's made you delusional? The other day you were crying because you and Alex had split. Now you're saying you're getting married!"

Sierra smiled patiently at her older sister. "That's

right. Alex and I have solved our differences. He proposed and I accepted. We want to get married quickly so we can start the adoption papers for Bowie right after."

"Oh." A tiny frown creased the middle of her forehead. "Well, this is great news. Surprising. But great." She smiled then and leaning forward placed a kiss on Sierra's cheek. "Congratulations, sis."

Sierra kissed her in return. "Thank you. But you don't sound all that happy about it to me."

Gloria waved a ringed hand through the air. "I am, Sierra, truly. But the part about Bowie. Are you sure you're not just marrying Alex so that you'll have a better chance of adopting? Maybe you're getting your feelings for Alex and Bowie all tangled up together."

Of course her feelings for the two men in her life were tangled together, Sierra thought. That's the way it was when a woman loved a man and their child.

"No, Gloria. I'm not marrying Alex just as a way to get Bowie. That would be—how could you think I could be so conniving? I love Alex. Very much."

She'd thought admitting such a thing to anyone would be hard to do, but now that she'd said it, she was amazed at how good it felt.

"Sierra, I wasn't suggesting you were doing anything conniving—you're the last person on earth who could use another person. I just want you to be sure that you're marrying Alex for the right reasons."

Her eyes misty, Sierra hugged her sister close. "I am, Gloria. I can't live without the man."

Gloria chuckled softly. "You must know what you're doing because that's exactly the way I feel about Jack. Have you told Mom and Dad yet? And does Christina know?"

"I called them all earlier this morning. Christina wanted to come with us to shop for the dress, but she had an important meeting at work. Mom is going to meet me later to talk about the church and the flowers and what we're going to do about a reception. I tried to tell her that we didn't need a reception, but she won't hear of it."

"Of course she won't hear of it. We Mendozas like to celebrate," Gloria said, then dropped Sierra's hand and hurried back behind the counter. "Just let me get my purse. We're going to shop for this wedding until we drop."

Sierra laughed. "What about your shop? You can't just close up."

"Watch me," Gloria retorted as she grabbed her handbag and motioned for Sierra to follow her to the door. Once there, she flipped a Closed sign toward the front of the glass. "My sister is only getting married once in her lifetime. I'm not going to miss any of it."

The week passed for Sierra like a blurred trip on a fairground ride. She was so busy planning the wedding during the day that she fell into bed at night so exhausted that she slept. Fitfully, but she did sleep. Which was somewhat better than the wide-awake nights she'd spent while she and Alex had been separated.

Since the two of them had decided to get married, Sierra had asked Alex if he would refrain from moving into the house until they were married. She wanted their reunion to be special and blessed. She wanted their wedding night to be the start of all their tomorrows.

Thankfully Alex had understood her needs and had used the week to pack up his apartment and deal with ending his lease. Once their brief honeymoon was over Trey and Mario were going to help him move what furniture he wanted to keep and his endless boxes of law books while Gayle had promised to help Sierra move things around so the two-story would have enough room to accommodate Alex's things.

At first, their longtime college buddies had been stunned to hear that Alex and Sierra were getting married. But once the initial shock wore off, they were all thrilled and confident that the couple would have a long, happy marriage.

But now that the wedding day was upon them, Sierra was quaking with uncertainty as she dressed for the ceremony. With everything inside her, she hoped their friends were right. More than anything, she wanted their marriage to be happy and long-lived, but could that really happen if Alex didn't love her? she wondered. Would the love she felt for him be enough to keep them together through the sad and trying times?

"Sierra, you look like you're about to go into the hospital for open heart surgery, instead of about to marry the man of your dreams," Christina said to her as she fastened a pearl choker around Sierra's neck. "Are you feeling okay? You're as white as your dress."

Sierra, her two sisters who were also her brides-maids, and her friend Gayle, who'd be standing as her maid of honor, were gathered in a small dressing room located in one of the lesson rooms at the back of St. Mary's church. For the past thirty minutes, a crowd of women wanting to wish her well had passed in and out of the room. But now things had quieted down and the only thing left to complete Sierra's readiness was attaching her veil.

"Christina, I can't look as white as my dress." From her seat on the dressing stool, Sierra tried to laugh at her image in the mirror in front of her. "I'm Hispanic, remember."

Gayle, who was standing to one side in a svelte, dark blue shift, surveyed the bride with an eagle eye. "Your sister is right," she said, shaking a finger at Sierra. "You look like you're about to be sentenced to the death chamber. Are you scared or worried about something?"

Shaking her head, she gave the two women a wob-bly smile. "I'm just nervous. Doesn't a bride have a right to be nervous?"

"Yes, but—" Christina started to reply but Sierra quickly interrupted her.

"Why are you looking for trouble?" she questioned crossly. "There's nothing wrong!"

Gloria rose from a folding chair where she'd been resting and walked over to where the two women were hovering over Sierra. "Christina, quit badgering her! For heaven's sake, it's her wedding day!"

"I'm not badgering her," Christina retorted. "I just want to understand why she's so panicky." She looked anxiously down at Sierra's tight features. "All right, honey, if you expect to walk down the aisle when they start playing the 'Wedding March,' then you'd better speak up. Otherwise, I'm not letting you out of this room."

"Christina!" Gayle scolded again. "There is something on Sierra's mind. I can see it," she said, agreeing with Christina's observations.

Sierra let out a weary sigh. "I don't know why you're doing this to me now—just a few minutes before the ceremony is supposed to start!"

"Because," Christina said gently as she laid a steadying hand on Sierra's shoulder. "When Daddy takes you by the arm and leads you down the aisle to Alex, we want you to be happy."

"I am happy. I'm just a little scared, that's all."

Gayle moved to Sierra's side and took her by the hand. "It's Alex, isn't it?" she asked with somber concern.

After a moment or two of looking into her dear friend's face, Sierra realized she couldn't hold up her front any longer. Nodding, she said, "Yes, it's Alex."

"Well, honey, to be honest, I'd be more than a little nervous if I was marrying him," Gayle reasoned. "He's gorgeous, but he's a handful. He's so damn alpha male that you never know what's going to come out of his mouth. And there's also the problem of women eyeing him like a piece of candy."

"No. No. It's nothing like that," Sierra said in a low, strained voice. "I—I'm just not sure that Alex cares for me enough. I mean, not enough to be marrying me."

Gloria groaned in loud disbelief. Christina made a

scolding noise with the tip of her tongue. Beyond the closed door, in the other part of the church, Sierra could hear the pianist playing "Tonight We Love." But tonight wasn't what she was worried about. It was tomorrow and all the tomorrows after that.

"Alex cares for you deeply, Sierra," Gayle said. "Next to you, I probably know him better than anyone else in this room. And I can see how happy you've made him."

"Caring for and loving someone are two entirely different things," Sierra countered.

"What makes you think Alex doesn't love you?" Gloria spoke up.

Sierra grimaced. "Because he's never told me so. I'm not even sure he believes in love like that between a man and a woman."

"Good Lord," Christina exclaimed. "Don't you think it's a little late to be worrying about that?"

Bending her head, she said, "It doesn't matter, really. Because I love Alex enough for the both of us."

"And you've told him that?" Gayle prodded.

Sierra lifted her head to look at all three women. "No. I couldn't. Not knowing how he feels, well, I don't want him to think I'm pressuring him. If he does fall in love with me, I want him to do it on his own. I want it to be real."

"But if he doesn't know how you feel," Gloria pointed out. "And—"

"You don't know how he feels," Christina finished. "Then the two of you are going to be going through this marriage as blind as bats. Your relationship can't thrive and grow if you're holding back your feelings."

Sierra's brown eyes darkened with shadows of doubt. "But what if he's only marrying me so that he can be Bowie's father? He loves the baby very much."

"And so do you," Gayle reasoned. "But let's face it, Alex is a stud. He doesn't have to marry you to get a son."

"That's right," Gloria said gently. "Alex is marrying you because he loves you. I'd bet some of Jack's money on that," she teased.

They all laughed and Sierra suddenly realized her sisters and friend were right. She had to be honest with Alex. And tonight she would be.

Her eyes misty, Sierra smiled at the three of them. "Okay, now that I know what I have to do, would someone help me with my veil?"

A few short minutes later, Sierra came out of the dressing room with her maid of honor and bridesmaids in tow. Her father was waiting for her in the vestibule and his proud, fatherly smile beamed from ear to ear when he spotted his daughter moving toward him.

Her wedding gown, a gift from her two sisters, was white, floor-length silk. The princess style was fashioned with a sweetheart neckline that dipped to a low V between her breasts and a gored skirt that flared out from her slender waist. The long sleeves of Chantilly lace narrowed down to a point atop her hand, which was shaking, in spite of the pep talk Gayle and her sisters had given her.

Adjusting her bouquet of white lilies and Texas bluebonnets, she slipped her arm through her father's and he leaned down and kissed her cheek.

"I have never seen you look more beautiful, my daughter. I wish you every happiness in the world. No one knows, more than me, how much you deserve it."

Afraid her eyes were going to fill with tears, she blinked rapidly and smiled up at him. "Thank you, Daddy," she whispered. "Thank you for always loving me."

Beyond the vestibule the "Wedding March" began to play and Sierra watched her father's brown eyes fill with tears.

"It's time to go, honey. Your man is waiting."

They moved forward to the entrance of the church, then stepped onto the aisle leading to the altar where candlelight flickered and white lilies draped an archway.

On either side of Sierra and her father, the pews of the small church were filled with family and friends, but she was only partially aware of the attending crowd.

Behind the filmy white layers of netting, her gaze was focused on Alex standing tall and handsome at the altar in a dark suit. His eyes were locked on her, as if there was no one else in the room, or even the world, and in that moment all she could think was how very much she loved him.

During the past week the Calloways had flown down from Dallas and met with Sierra's family. The Mendozas had kindly invited them to stay in their home until the wedding took place. Maria and Jose had also prepared a magnificent reception for the newlyweds at

Red. A live band played a variety of dance music and long tables were laden with some of the most delicious dishes the restaurant had to offer. An enormous tiered wedding cake, complete with bride and groom on top, finished off the celebration.

By the time the two of them were finally able to sneak away from the party, the sun was dipping low and they had less than an hour to make it to the airport in San Antonio.

During the flight south, Sierra drifted off to sleep with her hand wrapped in Alex's and her head resting on his shoulder. It was the first peaceful minute they'd had all day and though Alex tried to sleep, too, he couldn't close his eyes, much less think about sleeping.

Sierra was finally his wife. It was amazing how much that meant to him and how desperately he'd wanted their marriage to happen. He'd never thought he could feel this protective about any woman. He'd never believed he could want one so much, or love one so deeply.

It had taken Alex a long time to realize just how strong his feelings for Sierra were. Years, he supposed, because ever since their college days, something had always drawn him to her. Something had made him so frustrated with the boyfriends she'd dated. And he'd hated the way she was always caring for some downtrodden soul instead of herself.

That last thought put a wan smile on Alex's lips. Funny how that caring heart of hers was the very thing he adored about her now. Which only proved that love had the power to change a person.

Sierra groaned faintly in her sleep and Alex glanced down to study her face in the muted light. Her thick lashes rested like black crescent moons against her cheeks, her rosy-pink lips were slightly parted and so inviting even in slumber. The beauty of her features only made the unrest inside him whip up to all-out worry.

Sierra loved Bowie. He'd heard her say it time and again. No one had to tell him that she would do anything and everything to hold on to her baby. Did that also include marrying him? Alex wondered. Was that the only reason she'd accepted his proposal?

Maybe his fears were unwarranted, but he couldn't forget the fact that she'd never once mentioned love to him. Oh, she wanted him, just like he wanted her. But was that as far as it went with her? Sex and insurance that Bowie would finally be legally hers? Dear God, he didn't want to think that way. Especially on their wedding night.

But tonight was not his real worry, he realized. It was their future and if his love for Sierra was enough to keep her by his side.

Eventually the two of them landed in Brownsville and took a rental car to Padre Island. The hotel where they had reservations was located directly on the beach and the French doors in their room opened onto a balcony that looked out over the rolling gulf.

Sierra was entranced by the beautiful sight and kept repeating to Alex how wonderful he was to bring her to such a romantic place.

"Why wouldn't I bring you to a romantic place?" he teased as he stood beside her on the balcony, his arm draped loosely against the back of her waist. "Honeymoons aren't science field trips."

Laughing softly, she turned and slipped both arms around his waist. "Hmm. Just goes to prove a woman can learn something every day. So if we're not here on a field trip to catch butterflies, what are we going to do?"

"What a brazen hussy you are, Mrs. Calloway," he teased affectionately.

She smiled up at him and his heart caught as he watched the sea breeze tease her wet black curls and lift the ruffle of her low neckline. Only moments ago, she'd stepped out of the shower and Alex couldn't forget that underneath her thin robe was her beautiful naked body.

"It's you who made me this way," she said playfully.

Her robe was made of some sort of sheer fabric and the heat of her body warmed Alex's hands as he splayed them against her back and drew her forward.

"Hmm. Then I've done something right for once in my life." Bending his head, he gently settled his lips over hers. At the same time he felt her arms try to gather him closer, her lips part with hunger. The simple invitation was more than enough to fire his blood and he deepened the kiss until they were both heaving for air.

"Sierra," he said raggedly. "It's been hell not making love with you these past weeks. I didn't know I could hurt for someone the way I've hurt for you."

Her hands came up to cradle his face and she pushed

at the hank of hair the sea wind had blown into his eyes. "I've taken a few cold showers myself," she admitted.

Surprise arched his brows. "Really?"

She laughed softly and the sound buoyed his heart. If he could only hear that sound for the rest of his life, he'd die a happy man.

"Alex, surely, when we were together weeks back, you could see, feel how much I wanted you."

Wanted? What about loved? What's in that sweet, giving heart of yours, Sierra?

The questions were on the tip of Alex's tongue, but he bit them back with a groan that betrayed some of the anguish he was feeling.

"I hope you didn't waste money on one of those flimsy negligees. I don't want to wait while you lock yourself inside the bathroom and dress yourself up for me. You'll look beautiful enough with just this on," he said, lifting her left hand to his lips and kissing the gold band on her finger.

Her chuckle was more like a sexy growl. "I didn't bother buying any sort of sleepwear for our honeymoon. Not when I knew I'd only be wearing it for a few seconds."

"Come here, my wife." With a husky laugh, he picked her up and carried her to the bed.

Chapter Fourteen

A dim pool of light coming from the bedside lamp il-
luminated the king-size bed. After Alex had deposited
her on the edge of the mattress, he reached down and
clicked off the artificial light. Instantly the room was
bathed in soft moonlight and the silver glow reflecting
off the ocean.

Sierra watched him toss away his shirt and shorts and
then she stood, only inches in front of him, and loosened the tie at her waist. As soon as he touched her
shoulders, the flimsy material slid to the floor.

She could hear his breathing quicken as he reached
out and touched one breast and her pulse began to race
with sweet anticipation.

"Today when I saw you walking down the aisle toward me, I was certain you could never look more beautiful," he whispered. "But tonight you look like a goddess."

Smiling, she stepped closer and slid her hands down the planes of his shoulders. "That's because you turned out the light."

His hands closed around her waist and drew her against him. Sierra's blood began to sing as his hands cupped her buttocks and his arousal stirred against her belly.

"I can see just fine, Mrs. Calloway."

Rising on her tiptoes, she curled her arms around his neck and turned her lips to the side of his face. He quickly twisted his head to find her mouth and Sierra moaned with pleasure as his lips roamed greedily over hers.

Continuing the kiss, he nudged her backward until her calves hit the side of the bed, then, gently, he eased the both of them down on the mattress.

Once he broke the contact of their lips, they were both gulping for air and Alex whispered against the curve of her neck. "I need you so much—so much."

And she needed him for the rest of her life, she thought, as love swelled her heart to the bursting point.

"Let me do something about that," she murmured as desire began to grip her like a tight glove. She pushed at his shoulder until he was lying on his back and then she straddled his hips.

"Baby. Baby! You're too good to me," he muttered in a hoarse voice.

Leaning forward, she cupped her palm against his

cheek. "My husband," she whispered fervently, then, bending lower, she placed her lips over his.

With a growl of fierce need, Alex thrust himself inside her and let the hungry rhythm of her body carry him away.

Later, after the heat of their bodies had cooled, Alex drowsily stroked the back of Sierra's long hair.

"Alex?" She propped her head on her hand and studied his face in the moonlight.

"Hmm?"

"Let's go sit on the beach. There's something I want to talk to you about."

"The beach! Good Lord, woman, it's way past midnight, can't you talk right here? This bed feels awfully good, especially with you in it."

She slid a finger down the middle of his chest until she reached his navel. Once there, she hesitated, then dared to slip her hand a bit farther.

"Yeah, but just think how good it will feel to get back in it," she softly purred.

"God, I must have been out of my mind," he exclaimed good-naturedly as he rose up and flung the sheet off both their legs. "All these years I thought you were some meek little thing that got her kicks from books. Boy, did I have you pegged wrong."

Even though he was teasing, his comment thrilled Sierra. For a long time, even before she'd ever dreamed of having him for a lover, she'd wanted him to think of her as sexy and sultry and a woman who could turn a man's head and keep it turned. But when one man after another had left her flat and the last one had accused her of being boring, she'd doubted herself as a woman capable of attracting any man.

Now Alex made her feel beautiful and sensuous and wanted. If she tried to tell him in a million words how empowered that made her feel, he still wouldn't understand.

"You'll survive," she promised as she jerked on a pair of shorts and a halter top.

Seeing she wasn't about to relent on her purpose, Alex pulled on shorts and a shirt, leaving the latter unbuttoned to the muggy air.

The both of them stuck their feet in leather sandals before they exited the hotel through a side door away from the main lobby.

The night was very warm, the wind stiff. Alex noticed a half moon was suspended above the ocean and the silver light laced the tide as it rolled onto the wide beach. As he took Sierra by the hand and walked across the warm sand, he wondered how he could get through the days and months ahead without knowing if his wife loved him. If she'd simply married him to secure Bowie's adoption, he didn't know if he could stand it. Yet he had to, he realized. He loved her too much to do anything else.

"Do you think Bowie is okay?" she asked as they found a spot just out of reach of the tide and sank onto the sand. "I miss him so much."

He swallowed as uncertainty rolled around in the pit of his stomach. "I'm sure your mother is taking wonderful care of him. And if she needs help, you have two sisters who will be more than willing to lend a hand."

"Yes, but he's used to me. I know exactly how he likes to be rocked and fed—" She stopped suddenly and shook her head. "I'm sorry, Alex. I sound like a fretful mother. That's not what a groom wants to hear on his wedding night."

He rubbed the back of her hand with his thumb. "I want to hear anything you want to tell me."

Oh God, he was so dear, so much a part of her, she thought. If she said something wrong, if she got too emotional and caused a wedge between them now, she'd never be able to stand it.

Turning her face to the salty breeze, she shook back her hair and breathed deeply.

"Alex, I didn't ask you to come down here to talk about Bowie. I think I'm pretty sure you understand how much I love him. And I'm fairly certain that you love him, too."

Still holding on to her fingers, he slipped his opposite hand around the back of her waist. "That is the reason I'm making him my son."

She released another shaky breath. "He's important to both of us."

"That's probably an understatement," he said gently, then, studying her face, he shook his head. "Darlin', why are you looking so serious? It's a gorgeous night. We're on the beach and we have each other all to ourselves."

Lifting her chin, she gave him a quavering smile. "You're right. This night is so special." She lifted her hand and touched her fingers to his cheek. "That's why I—oh, Alex, promise that you won't laugh or ridicule me when I tell you this—"

"Sierra," he gently interrupted. "No one has to tell me I'm a stinker at times. But I won't laugh. Unless you tell me a joke."

But maybe he would think it was a joke, Sierra thought sickly. All these years he'd mostly used the word "love" as a sarcastic verb.

"Alex, the real reason I married you is—"

Terrified at what she was about to tell him, he touched a finger to her lips. "Before you say anything else, I have to tell you something. I—"

"Alex, don't keep interrupting me!" she scolded gently. "I'm trying to tell you that I love you!"

Her outburst caught him totally off guard and he stared at her for long moments. "Oh God. Oh, Sierra!"

His hands came up to cradle the back of her head and he tilted her face upward to the moonlight.

Her expression puzzled, she asked, "Alex, what are you doing?"

"I'm looking at you with your face bathed in moonlight and your hair whipping like strands of glossy silk. I want to always remember you just like this."

Sierra's heart was beating so hard and fast she thought it was going to burst from her chest. "Why?"

The corners of his mouth tilted to a satisfied grin. "Because you're my wife. The woman I love."

It took a moment for her to digest his declaration, but once she did, a whimper passed her lips and she fell forward and buried her face against his bare chest.

"Alex," she said through happy tears. "All this time I've been afraid to tell you how I felt—because I was certain you could never love me. I thought—I was afraid you were only marrying me because you wanted to be Bowie's father."

He laughed as a joy such as he'd never felt before zinged through his veins and pumped sheer happiness straight into his heart. "Oh, Sierra, you're not going to believe this. But I thought the same thing about you. I figured you were only marrying me because your chances of adopting Bowie would be much better with a father in the house."

Her cheeks wet with happy tears, she flung her arms around his neck and clung tightly. "We've been crazy, Alex."

"Yeah. And we'll probably be crazy again. But we'll get through it. Together. Always together." Easing her head back, he placed a long, promising kiss upon her lips that left her sighing with contentment.

"What do you think about starting on a brother or sister for Bowie? He'll need several, you know," he said with a sly grin. "Or do you want to wait until we're married longer?"

Why would she want to wait? Sierra wondered blissfully. They'd already had nine years together. She knew he'd be around for the next nine and for always after that.

"Actually I've got to admit something, Alex. For the first time ever, I forgot to take my birth control pill this morning. I guess I was just too excited with wedding preparations to remember. Maybe now is a good time to toss the rest of them in the trash?"

Laughing, he tugged her up from their seats on the sand and pulled her along toward the roaring surf.

"Uh, don't you think that project would work better if we went back to bed?" she asked.

"Later."

"Alex!" she squealed as water rushed over her feet. "What are you doing?"

"We're going to take a little swim."

"Now?" she asked incredulously. "What about the bed?"

Laughing, he teased, "Just think how good it will feel once we get back in it."

Epilogue

Sierra didn't waste any time about paying off her debt to her sisters. The next weekend after she and Alex had come home from their honeymoon, she offered herself to Christina and Gloria as their happy slave.

Since either sister couldn't think of any task they considered awful enough to punish Sierra for going back on her word and marrying a man, she suggested they allow her to cook each one of them a nice dinner. She even managed to add a shudder, as though the very thought was downright horrible.

Let them think they were punishing her, Sierra thought, as she happily hummed to herself in Christina's kitchen. She loved to cook and because she did so much of it, she was very efficient in the kitchen.

Yesterday had been Gloria's payday and Sierra had pretended to kill herself over a huge pot roast dinner. She wasn't about to tell her sisters that she'd read a paperback while the whole thing was cooking in the oven.

Today, for Christina, she was preparing steak fajitas. What could be easier than stir-frying a few strips of meat, peppers and onions and rolling it all up in warm tortillas, she thought with a clever giggle.

"Hey, I thought this was supposed to be a chore for you," Christina suddenly spoke from out of nowhere. "Instead you're laughing. If you think it's so funny, maybe Gloria and I should put you outside mowing the lawn."

Christina wasn't supposed to be back in the house for another hour. The sound of her voice shocked Sierra and she whirled around from the sizzling skillet to see both her sisters standing in the middle of the kitchen, eyeing her with amused but accusing looks.

Laughing sheepishly, Sierra waved a dismissive hand in the air and tried to appear as weary as possible. "Oh, you two are really mean. I wasn't laughing about the cooking. In fact, I'm just exhausted from standing over this hot stove. I don't know why Christina made me do all this frying!"

"Uh-huh," Gloria said with a pointed smile. "Everybody laughs when they're exhausted."

Sierra's mind grabbed on to the first feasible excuse that popped into her head. "For your information, dear sisters, I was laughing because I'm so happy. Alex and I received some great news this morning."

"Oh? What?" Christina quickly prompted. She walked over to the cabinet and picked up a strip of raw bell pepper and chomped into the piece of vegetable.

Sierra's brown eyes were suddenly lit from within and the glow spread to her entire face. "We'll be signing the adoption papers for Bowie on Tuesday."

"That soon!" Gloria exclaimed. "I thought there'd be weeks of red tape. Even with Alex using his legal prowess."

"So did we," Sierra explained. "Alex and I both expected a long process. But he has friends in high places. One of the state legislators owed him a favor and he pulled some strings. The papers will be ready for us to sign in a couple days. And then you two can help me plan a christening party."

"Oh, Sierra, that's the greatest news!" Christina cried with joy.

"Absolutely wonderful!" Gloria added as both sisters rushed to hug Sierra tightly.

After a few moments of happy tears and congratulations, Sierra disentangled herself from the two women and turned back to her skillet before the whole meal was burned to a crisp.

Christina and Gloria grabbed cold sodas from the fridge and sat down at a nearby table. Both women kicked off their heels and sighed with pleasure as they wiggled squished toes.

After a moment Christina looked at Gloria and winked. "Sierra, there's flour all over that cute little nose of yours. You'd better be careful and not sneeze. Your nostrils might glue together."

"Very funny," Sierra drawled. "That's what I get for making you homemade tortillas. See what I ever do for you again." Glancing over her shoulder, she arched a brow at her sisters. "So what have you two been doing, out trying to make up nasty jokes about your sister's cooking?"

Laughing, Gloria reached down and rubbed her aching calves. "Not hardly. We've been out all day shopping for evening dresses."

Surprised, Sierra looked back and forth between the two of them. "Evening dresses," she repeated blankly. "What's the occasion, Fortune-Rockwell is throwing some sort of shindig?"

Christina rose from her chair and twirled around on the ball of her bare foot. "It's much more exciting than that. Governor Meyers is throwing a party and we're invited."

Sierra raised her brows to mocking proportions. "Oh, I didn't realize you two were chummy with the governor."

Gloria laughed. "We're not. But we're friends with Ryan Fortune and the governor happens to think Ryan deserves a party for all of the charitable deeds he's done for our area."

"He certainly does deserve it," Sierra said matter-of-factly. "So did you two find something to wear?"

"Not yet," Christina told her. "We're going to look again tomorrow. Want to come with us?"

Sierra tossed her sisters a wry smile. "Why would I want to go? I don't need an evening dress."

"Oh, yes, you do," Gloria spoke up. "You and Alex are invited, too. But come to think of it, you look pretty cute in that getup you're cooking in. Maybe you just ought to wear that."

Sierra glanced down at her flour-and-grease splotched T-shirt and jeans, then burst out laughing.

Giggling along with her, Gloria and Christina left their seats to join her and all three women hugged together in a tight, loving circle. They were truly a family again.

* * * * *

You won't want to miss Signature Select's new twelve-book series,
THE FORTUNES OF TEXAS: REUNION,
which features your favorite family!
Ann Major launches the series with
COWBOY AT MIDNIGHT—
available June 2005.

For a sneak preview, turn the page!

Prologue

The Double Crown Ranch

Somebody was going to die!

Rosita Perez *knew* this as she sprang forward in her bed and threw off her sheets and cotton quilt; she *knew* it by the swift darts of pain that made her left breast ache.

The room felt as icy as a meat locker. Even so, her long black hair with its distinctive white streak above her forehead was soaking wet, as was her pillow. Hot flashes, her gringo doctor would say.

Smart gringo doctors thought they knew everything. She *knew* better.

Somebody was going to die. Somebody close at hand.

Rosita was descended from a long line of *curanderos*. Since birth she'd been cursed, or blessed, with the sight. Like her ancestors, who'd been natural healers, she saw things; she felt things that other people didn't feel.

Life wasn't lived on a single plane. Nor was the world and its machinations entirely logical, much as her bosses, Ryan and Lily Fortune, might like to think. She'd learned to keep her visions to herself because most people, even her beloved husband, Ruben, didn't believe her.

After pulling on her robe, she tiptoed out of the bedroom and down the hall, taking care not to wake Ruben. A light from outside beckoned her and she headed for the front windows of her living room.

The red glow in the sky above the ranch made her shake even more. Sensing evil, she felt too afraid to go out on her front porch.

Which was ridiculous. She'd faced cougars and bobcats and convicts on the loose while living alone on the ranches. Despite her misgivings, no, because of them, she opened the front door and forced herself to pad bravely out onto the porch of her ranch house.

Help! The cry was silent and it came from nowhere, and yet from everywhere. The plaintive wail consumed her soul. Sensing death, she sucked in a breath and stared at the dark fringe of trees that circled her home like prison walls.

"Who are you?" she whispered.

A blood-red moon the exact shade of the skull in her

nightmare hung over the ranch. Circling it was a bright scarlet ring. She stared and stared, aware that the dense night smelled sweetly of juniper and buzzed with the music of millions of cicadas.

Summer smells. Summer sounds. Why did they make her feel terrible tonight?

She kept watching the moon until it vanished behind a black cloud. She wasn't feeling any easier when a bunch of coyotes began to hoot and she heard a man's eerie laughter from beyond the juniper long after they stopped.

"Who's out there?" she cried.

The cicadas stopped their serenade. A thousand eyes seemed to stare at her from the thick wall of dark trees.

Had someone heard her? Stark fear drained the blood from her face.

With a muted cry, she raced back inside her brilliantly lit living room with its dozens of velvet floral paintings and comforting overstuffed furniture. Not that she felt comforted tonight.

Slamming her door, she stared unseeingly at the sofa piled high with her recent purchases from a flea market—mirror sunglasses, towel set, children's clothes and toys, all in need of sorting.

Maybe the moon hadn't been a human skull, but one thing was for sure—she'd never seen anything like that blood-red moon circled with a ring of fire before. Never in all her sixty-six years.

And the laughter… that terrible, inhuman laughter…
Someone was out there.

Rosita could trace her blood to prehistoric civilizations in Mexico. She knew in her bones that such a moon meant things didn't bode well.

The Fortunes were in trouble—again.

She'd worked for them for a long time. Too long, Ruben said. He wanted her to retire, so she could focus on him. "We'll move away, not too far, but we'll have a place of our own."

Ruben had always wanted his own land, but she loved Ryan Fortune and his precious wife, Lily, as if they were members of her own family. She couldn't leave them. Not now! Not when she knew they needed her more than ever. In the morning she would try to warn them as she cooked them eggs, bacon, tamales and frijoles. She cooked frijoles with every meal.

They would probably laugh at her and tease her as they always did. They'd waited so long to realize their love. They wanted to be happy, and she wanted that for them, too. With the sun high in the sky, maybe she would be able to laugh and hope all would be well.

She made a fist. "I have to tell them anyway! First thing, when I go to the ranch house!"

When she finally stopped shaking, it was a long time before she felt safe enough to switch off the light. Even then she was still too restless to go back to bed or to sort through her flea market purchases, so she curled up in her favorite armchair and let the rosy-tinted darkness wrap her while she waited for the sun to come up and chase her ghosts away.

If only she could wake Ruben and tell him about the skull and the laughter.

But he would only think her stupid, tell her it was nothing and order her to bed.

"*Ya veràs.* You'll see, *viejo.* You'll see, she whispered.

Then she shivered as the shadowy forms of the tall furniture in her living room shaped themselves into snakes and cougars and alligators.

Somebody was going to die!

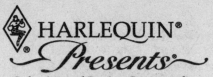

HARLEQUIN®
Presents~

Seduction and Passion Guaranteed!

GREEK TYCOONS

They're the men who have everything—
except brides…

Wealth, power, charm—what else could a
heart-stoppingly handsome tycoon need?
In the GREEK TYCOONS miniseries you have
already been introduced to some gorgeous Greek
multimillionaires who are in need of wives.

**Now it's the turn of favorite Presents
author Lucy Monroe,
with her attention-grabbing romance**

THE GREEK'S INNOCENT VIRGIN
Coming in May
#2464

www.eHarlequin.com   HPTGIV

HARLEQUIN®
Presents

Seduction and Passion Guaranteed!

Introducing a brand-new trilogy by

Sharon Kendrick

Passion, power & privilege – the dynasty continues
with these handsome princes...

Welcome to Mardivino—a beautiful and wealthy
Mediterranean island principality, with a prestigious
and glamorous royal family. There are three
Cacciatore princes—Nicolo, Guido and
the eldest, the heir, Gianferro.

Next month (May 05), meet Nico in

THE MEDITERRANEAN
PRINCE'S PASSION #2466

Coming in June: Guido's story, in

THE PRINCE'S LOVE-CHILD #2472

Coming soon: Gianferro's story in

THE FUTURE KING'S BRIDE

Only from Harlequin Presents

www.eHarlequin.com

HPRHC

If you enjoyed what you just read,
then we've got an offer you can't resist!

Take 2 bestselling love stories FREE!

Plus get a FREE surprise gift!

Clip this page and mail it to Silhouette Reader Service™

IN U.S.A.	IN CANADA
3010 Walden Ave.	P.O. Box 609
P.O. Box 1867	Fort Erie, Ontario
Buffalo, N.Y. 14240-1867	L2A 5X3

YES! Please send me 2 free Silhouette Special Edition® novels and my free surprise gift. After receiving them, if I don't wish to receive anymore, I can return the shipping statement marked cancel. If I don't cancel, I will receive 6 brand-new novels every month, before they're available in stores! In the U.S.A., bill me at the bargain price of $4.24 plus 25¢ shipping and handling per book and applicable sales tax, if any*. In Canada, bill me at the bargain price of $4.99 plus 25¢ shipping and handling per book and applicable taxes**. That's the complete price and a savings of at least 10% off the cover prices—what a great deal! I understand that accepting the 2 free books and gift places me under no obligation ever to buy any books. I can always return a shipment and cancel at any time. Even if I never buy another book from Silhouette, the 2 free books and gift are mine to keep forever.

235 SDN DZ9D
335 SDN DZ9E

Name	(PLEASE PRINT)	
Address	Apt.#	
City	State/Prov.	Zip/Postal Code

Not valid to current Silhouette Special Edition® subscribers.

Want to try two free books from another series?
Call 1-800-873-8635 or visit www.morefreebooks.com.

* Terms and prices subject to change without notice. Sales tax applicable in N.Y.
** Canadian residents will be charged applicable provincial taxes and GST.
  All orders subject to approval. Offer limited to one per household.
  ® are registered trademarks owned and used by the trademark owner and or its licensee.

SPED04R   ©2004 Harlequin Enterprises Limited